Publish and
Be Killed

Also by Anne Morice:

ANNE MORICE

Publish and Be Killed

St. Martin's Press
New York

Library of Congress Cataloging in Publication Data

Morice, Anne.
   Publish and be killed.

   I. Title.
PR6063.0743P8   1987   823'.914   86-24778
ISBN 0-312-00178-9

First published in Great Britain by Macmillan London Limited.

First U.S. Edition

10 9 8 7 6 5 4 3 2 1

Publish and
Be Killed

ONE

'Derek has a tale to unfold,' Robin said late one Friday evening, 'which I think may interest you. Or are you too tired?'

'No, not at all,' I replied untruthfully.

It was then creeping up towards midnight and already an hour had passed since he arrived home, accompanied by Detective Sergeant Derek Haworth, who had been all too easily persuaded to step inside and round off the evening with a drink.

However, I tried to assume an alert and receptive expression because I liked Derek, who was a solid, chunky young man, with true blue eyes and, according to Robin, many sterling qualities to compensate for a certain lack of humour. I also recognised and understood their urge to prolong the occasion to the point where the last member of the audience fell asleep.

They had returned to London after five gruelling days in the north of England, in pursuit of a particularly cunning and repellent murderer, who had managed to evade capture for over a year. The operation had been brought to a successful and unbloody conclusion and they were both in that state of mind which I had sometimes experienced myself after a rapturous opening night, having reached the pitch of exhaustion where, in defiance of common sense and better judgement, they could not resist the temptation to savour their triumph for just a few more minutes.

'Is it a crime story?' I asked, making an effort not to sound like Nanny in an indulgent mood.

'No, although it does have ingredients which might yet

5

turn it into one,' Robin said, 'which is one reason why we thought you might be interested. Also Derek wants your opinion.'

'Oh, you mean an idea for a script?'

'No, not that either. In fact, it's the prospect of its getting into print which is causing alarm. Go on, Derek, you tell her!'

'Yes, all right, but it means starting a good way back, I'm afraid. Can you bear it?'

Since it was obviously not going to matter whether I could or not, I nodded and Derek went on:

'The thing is, you see, I have to explain about Pam's family and it's rather complicated. You remember that Pam and I got married just over a year ago?'

'Yes, indeed I do. I'm sorry I couldn't get to your wedding, but I was in Coventry with Strindberg at the time. I met Pam when you brought her here one evening, though, and I thought she was lovely.'

'Thank you. We're expecting our first baby in February.'

'Congratulations!'

'But February is six months away,' Robin reminded him, 'and I think we'll get on faster if you take things in the right order.'

'Okay, I'll do my best, although the baby does have some bearing on it, as you know. Where was I?'

'You were going to tell me about Pam's family,' I said, 'although I can't see that my opinion on that subject is likely to be much use to you. To be honest, I can't even remember her maiden name.'

'Tilling. Pam Tilling and her mother is called Laura Tilling. If you had been at the wedding, you might just possibly have recognised her.'

'Laura Tilling? No...no, I don't think so. The name does sound familiar, for some reason, but I'm sure I've never met her. Was she on the stage, by any chance?'

'Sort of, when she was quite young, but she's better known as a writer of historical novels.'

'Oh yes, of course! Laura Tilling! That's how I know the name.'

'Two of her sisters made brief appearances on the stage too and there are strong theatrical connections in the family. In both families, come to that.'

'Oh God, Derek, it must be later than I thought, or else I'm very dense. Have we really been talking about two families?'

'It's Derek's fault,' Robin assured me. 'I think he may be trying to grab your interest with these enigmatic asides. Come on, now, Derek, just stick to plain facts.'

'Yes, sorry. The point being, Tessa, that before Laura married Pam's father her name was Lampeter. Her mother was Kitty Lampeter. Does that mean anything to you?'

I cudgelled my tired brain into making a quick calculation before I answered.

'Meaning that your grandfather-in-law was that celebrated old Edwardian playwright, Sheridan Seymour?'

'Correct!'

'Who had three children, or was it four, by Kitty Lampeter, to whom he was never married?'

'There were three, as it happens. Laura, her elder sister, Rita, who married young and went to live in Ireland, where her husband trains horses, and finally Tom. He was born after them and after all three of the Seymour half-sisters on the legitimate side.'

'Well, don't worry,' I told him, relieved to have found it such a smooth ride after all, 'your secret is safe with me and about ten thousand other people.'

'So many, after all these years?'

'I daresay not all the names and details are remembered and they would probably be mostly people in a certain category and age group. If you were to mention any of the characters to forty people in a bus queue, you'd probably

7

get no response at all, but gossip dies hard in the theatre, you know. And, after all, what does it matter? Illegitimacy carries no stigma now and there are some who maintain that old Sheridan would have left his wife and married Kitty like a shot if it hadn't spoilt his chances of getting a knighthood. I gather she was a great beauty, with loads of charm, but of course adultery in those days was much more acceptable than divorce and both women seem to have accepted the situation very gracefully.'

'Yes, they did. In fact, they were close friends and remained so after Sheridan died, which speaks well for both of them, I've always thought.'

'And now they're both dead too, so why on earth should you and Pam be worrying about something which was over so many years ago?'

'Unfortunately, it may not be quite over. There are signs that it is about to be resuscitated.'

'Yes, well, I understand that does happen every so often. Apparently, the Seymour girls were always getting mixed up in slightly unsavoury scandals and making asses of themselves in two continents in their heyday. And wasn't there some furore over Sheridan's will ten or twelve years ago? I remember hearing people discuss it, but I've forgotten the details.'

'Derek will now remind you,' Robin said.

'Remind away, Derek!'

'He left the bulk of his capital to his son out of wedlock, Pam's uncle Tom.'

'Ah yes, the one and only boy among five sisters and half-sisters.'

'It wasn't so unfair as it sounds. All the Seymour girls had expensive educations, which the others, including Tom, certainly did not. Also they'd all been married at least once by the time their father died and collected a lot of money along the way, in addition to marriage settlements. Frances, Lady Seymour that is, was not at all

8

put out. She'd always been well off in her own right, which is probably why Sheridan married her in the first place. In fact, Pam's mother always believed that it was Frances who persuaded him to leave his money in that way. She considered that the Lampeters had had a rotten deal during his lifetime, while her own lot were being showered with every luxury under the sun.'

'Frances may not have cared,' I said, 'but someone else obviously did. Or why all the uproar?'

'You bet your life someone did. All three of them, in fact. None of the Seymour ladies appears to have inherited their mother's generosity and they ganged up and contested the will. The youngest was the ringleader, of course, the one they still call Baba, believe it or not. The other two are known as Angie and Dodie, short for Dorothy.'

'Why do you say "of course Baba was the ringleader"?'

'Because she's the brightest and greediest of the lot. Always has been.'

'Did they win their case?'

'No, there was no reason why they should have. Sheridan was in his right mind and they were all handsomely provided for.'

'So what did Uncle Tom do with his windfall?'

'It wasn't an enormous sum. The old boy's popularity was on the wane by then and what there was didn't do Tom much good. He blewed the lot in about three years.'

'On riotous living?'

'Worse than that. It might at least have given the poor chap a run for his money, which is the exact reverse of what he got.'

'How do you mean?'

'The silly fool was stuck with the idea that his father hadn't made him his heir simply because he was the only boy, but because he was the only one of the family to have inherited the Seymour talent and he set about writing

9

some plays to prove it. They were hopelessly bad, I gather, but he had such faith in his own genius that he was quite willing to put up the money to finance them and there were enough sharks around who were keen to take some of it off him. He actually managed to get three of them put on in obscure little theatres outside London. They all sank without a trace, needless to say, and so that was that. He drifted along doing dead-end jobs for a few years, hospital orderly and things like that, and finished up by joining one of those pseudo-religious groups. He married some woman of the same persuasion, Beryl she's called and she was a nurse in the hospital where he worked. After that he virtually cut himself off from the rest of the family.'

'Why's that? Don't they approve of her?'

'Boot's on the other foot, I think. According to Laura, Beryl was the one who did the cutting off, particularly the Lampeter branch. I gather she did invite Baba and the other two Seymour half-sisters to the wedding, but you can imagine what sort of response that brought. So, having got her come-uppance there, she won't have any more to do with any of them and won't allow Tom to either.'

'Where do they live, do you know?'

'In some squalid little bungalow somewhere near Brighton, I believe.'

'Clogs to evangelism in one generation,' Robin remarked.

'Yes, how true, because Sheridan Seymour wasn't his real name, was it, Derek?'

'No, no, he was Cyril Smirke from Bermondsey, but he looked like the popular idea of an aristocrat, which was a help, and he'd always meant to have his name in lights, so he thought he might as well pick a good one while he was about it. The next thing, of course, was to marry someone out of a genuine top drawer and then he was really on his way.'

10

'You're a bit hard on him,' I protested, this raking over past theatrical history having banished fatigue. 'His plays are dated now because the world he was writing about has ceased to exist, if it ever did, but they were clever in their way, and witty too.'

'Yes, so Pam's told me. I've never seen one, myself. She also will have it that they're not nearly so reverent towards the nobility and gentry as people nowadays seem to imagine. The idols sometimes turn out to have feet of clay.'

'I don't find that surprising. Just an example of the leopard not being able to paint over all the spots simply by aspiring to become a lion.'

'This is all most fascinating and instructive,' Robin said, 'but isn't it time Derek told you what's on his mind and why he needs your advice?'

'Yes, I'd forgotten about that. Go ahead, Derek!'

'I was coming to it anyway because, now we've got all the background in place, I can give you the latest chapter in the saga and the villain, as usual, is dear old Baba, or the Marchioness of Doverfield, as she still insists on being called, despite the fact that she's been through two husbands since then. Hell hath no fury like a Seymour woman deprived of what she regards as her birthright and Baba's resentment has never cooled down. She has written her memoirs and we hear that they will be published in the spring. Round about the time when our baby is due, to make everything more complicated.'

'Why? Is it likely to affect him or her in some way?'

'More than likely seeing that the principal victim will probably be my mother-in-law. Pam is devoted to her and depends on her almost to an abnormal degree, I sometimes think. It was what they call a broken home, you see. Laura divorced her husband when Pam was five or six and ever since then they've been practically inseparable. Any emotional stress at a time like this wouldn't help to create the placid and serene sort of confinement we'd been hoping for.'

'But what sort of emotional stress are we talking about? How could Baba have anything new or shocking to reveal at this late stage? She can't have any illusions about getting the will revoked now?'

'No, that's not her game. She simply wants to get her own back and the way she has found for it is to produce evidence that neither Tom nor Laura was her father's child. In order to do that, she is about to reveal that Kitty, their mother, was not the selfless, devoted woman she conned everyone into believing, but a cheap whore who was having affairs on the side with dozens of other men and tricked Seymour into accepting someone else's bastard child as his own.'

'But what sort of evidence could she possibly produce to back up such a preposterous claim?'

'She says she has letters to prove it.'

'Oh, does she, now? Although, since you obviously believe them, if they exist at all, to be forgeries, why not sue her for libel, slander, speaking ill of the dead, malice aforethought and anything else that your police training might suggest?'

'And who do you suppose would win that battle? Her sole object is to get as much publicity as she possibly can for her foul accusations. A lawsuit would more or less ensure that she achieved it. It would probably increase her sales no end.'

'It might give a small boost to the Laura Tilling sales too,' I remarked. 'We shouldn't overlook that.'

'Yes, we should,' Robin said. 'As well as being trite and quite unworthy of you, a scandal of that sort would inevitably damage her reputation. She doesn't write the kind of books, let me remind you, which have Queen Elizabeth the First springing out of bed and brushing away a nostalgic tear for the dear old carefree days at Hatfield.

12

They're all carefully researched and completely unsensational.'

'A situation which is made trickier still,' Derek added, 'by the fact that she's beginning to build up a small success with them and recently gave a television interview, which included some anecdotes about her ancestry and childhood. It was all so long ago that she saw no harm in it when the interviewer probed her on the subject. The Tilling credibility won't exactly be enhanced by rumours that her mother was a promiscuous old harlot, with an eye to the main chance. It never matters in the end whether such stories are proved to be false or not, as you must know so well. Something always sticks.'

'I suppose so and it's a very nasty business. What puzzles me, though, is what spoke either of you imagines I might be able to put in Baba's wheel.'

It was curious because during the preceding ten or fifteen minutes we seemed imperceptibly to have switched roles. Presumably there had been a point where we had met on equal ground, but if so it must have passed too rapidly to have been noticed. Thereafter I had continued on the ascent and was now in a mood to prolong the conversation for another hour and a half, whereas the other two had been drifting steadily into somnolence and Derek responded to my last question with such a huge and heavy yawn that it took him a moment or two to regain enough breath to speak at all.

'Oh, sorry about that, Tessa! This has been quite a day and I'm not any longer sure that I'm up to explaining that part. Perhaps I could leave it to Robin to do it? He'd make a better job of it and it was his idea in the first place. I'd better be making tracks now. Pam promised on her oath not to try and stay awake for me, but you can't depend on her. Good night and thanks for putting up with me so nobly.'

* * *

13

'What was your idea in the first place?' I asked Robin, who was also now yawning his way towards oblivion.

'Oh, nothing much. Nothing for you to get steamed up about. The fact is, he started yammering on about all this in the car coming home, I wasn't particularly helpful and I wasn't deeply interested, to be honest, so I said he'd better come in and talk to you about it. I thought it belonged rather more in your sphere than mine and that you might have something practical to suggest, but the main thing was to give him a chance to unburden himself.'

'It sounds to me as though my latest job is to provide that extra bit of therapy for overtired, but otherwise sane and efficient sergeants. Is that the idea?'

'Certainly not, there's nothing neurotic about Derek, if that's what you're hinting. He's extremely clear-sighted on most subjects. He just happens to be besotted about his rather tiresome wife. If that requires therapy, I suppose I must be overdue for treatment myself.'

'I'm prepared to accept that as a backhanded compliment,' I told him. 'At least, I think I am, but I'll let you know for certain in the morning. What sort of tiresome is Pam? She seemed quite a dim sort of girl the one and only time I met her.'

'She has hidden shallows. However, we can talk about that tomorrow too. I still have a few bits and pieces to tidy up on this case, so I'll have left before you're awake, but with any luck I'll be home for lunch and have the rest of the weekend off.'

'Good for you!' I told him. 'You left the best bit to the last.'

14

TWO

On Saturday morning, as early as I decently could, which was at ten thirty precisely, I telephoned my old friend Clarissa Jones, who was then appearing in a revival at the Haymarket, to ask if she could get me the house seats for the early performance.

'I couldn't say, I'm sure,' she replied haughtily. 'They are in high demand. We're doing rattling good business, you may be surprised to hear.'

'Yes, I had heard and no one could be more delighted than me, Clarrie dear. All the same, I thought maybe on a Saturday afternoon in August it might slacken off a bit. Still, no matter. I'd gladly pay for stalls any day of the week to see you in fringes and bangles, with a bandeau round your head and a long cigarette holder. Just be an angel and fix it with the box office for me. I'll pick them up five minutes before the curtain.'

'I can't think why it is, Tessa, that you always have to ring up practically in the middle of the night to reel off your instructions. How many do you want?'

'Only two. There's a good chance that Robin will be able to come with me.'

'Oh, that'll be nice,' she said, sounding more co-operative, 'and will you bring him round to see me afterwards?'

'Of course. We might even take you out for a cup of tea and a bun.'

'Oh, lovely! Something to look forward to! Bye for now, duckie. I need my sleep, even if you don't.'

There was no need for further reminders about tickets,

for I knew her of old and the mention of Robin had ensured that the matter would not be overlooked. It was not that she had any particular designs on him, in so far as she would not have gone to any great lengths to detach him from his tiresome wife. On the other hand, nor would she have hesitated to do so, if the opportunity had presented itself, because that was the way she was made. The product of a spartan upbringing in a freezing Midlands parsonage, she had reacted in the classic style by running away at an early age in order to live life to the full and indulge in every excess which had been forbidden at home. Having wisely chosen the stage as the shortest route to this goal and invested every penny of her post office savings account in a down payment for a drama course, she had been well on her way to achieving it before the end of her first term.

It was not that she had been blessed with any special talent, still less the will or capacity for hard work, but such was her alluring beauty, combined with the indefinable gift known as star quality, that, from her first audition, everyone who saw her had recognised Clarrie as one of Nature's knock-outs. The verdict had been borne out too and, had she only applied herself a little more earnestly to her craft and kept her tempestuous private life more firmly under control, she might have become one of the great international stars of her generation. Such disciplines were foreign to her, however, and she had no wish to acquire them. She might complain from morning till night, and often did, about whichever husband or lover happened to be currently in possession of her heart, but that was really how she liked it. It was the histrionics of the boudoir, not the public theatre, which kept her tuned up to crash through life with eyes peeled for the next conquest.

The play she was now appearing in, which was called *A Woman of Low Repute*, could have been written for her, had she been born eighty years earlier. It had been the first and least successful Sheridan Seymour play to be performed in London and had had only one subsequent revival. Sheridan had profited from the experience, which had taught him that, while his audiences might be willing to accept the premise that a woman without breeding could, in a crisis, display more courage and integrity than her so-called betters, they would do so more readily if the so-called betters were not depicted as utterly deficient in these qualities. Thereafter he had been sedulous in loading the dice more evenly, but in recent years fashions and attitudes had changed and present-day critics and audiences had hailed this play as being years ahead of its time and had discovered in Sheridan Seymour, of all improbable people, an important social influence of his period. The run, originally limited to three months, had now been extended to five and, for once, Clarrie had not exaggerated when she said that business was brisk. On Saturday afternoon the house was almost full, a surge of excitement was running through the crush of people in the foyer, and the confusion and turmoil made it almost impossible for us to battle our way through the long queue at the advance booking office.

'Those Seymour ladies must be making a bomb,' I remarked, as the house lights went up for the interval.

'How come?' Robin asked.

'Well, look at it! How often do you find this kind of scene at an August matinee?'

'Yes, it's obviously making a packet for someone, but I was under the impression that the copyright would have expired when the author had been dead for so long. I hadn't realised that his heirs could benefit indefinitely.'

'They can't, but that time hasn't quite come for this lot. Another few years to go, I should imagine. The old man was comparatively obscure during the last two decades of his life, but he hasn't been dead all that long. Also I've been told that Baba got herself a very sharp young agent to

17

handle things when the plays started picking up again and she was back in business. He's up to all the tricks and has probably got a very decent percentage for her; and for himself, too, incidentally, with his ten per cent of the royalties.'

'There now! You seem to be a good deal better informed on the subject than you admitted last night.'

'I am, but that, as you say, was last night. I've had twelve hours to busy myself on the telephone and I'm now up to the minute.'

'It was kind of you to go to so much trouble, but, as I've told you, I don't think Derek seriously expected you to take up the cudgels in any practical way. He was wound up and looking for a sympathetic and understanding ear. You provided it and that was enough.'

'It may have been enough for him, but sympathetic ears don't necessarily go into limbo when the conversation ends. The chase is on now and until something more rewarding or amusing turns up I mean to keep going.'

'Then I can only hope that something more rewarding or amusing has turned up by this time tomorrow. Judging on your past record, any murky situation which you start peering into has been known, as often as not, to end with someone getting killed. Then we might have to decide whether Pam murdered Baba in order to spare her mother humiliation and ridicule, or whether Laura murdered her to save Pam from a miscarriage and nervous breakdown. Neither outcome would do much to further Derek's career.'

'You seem to be under the impression, Robin, that I create a climate for murder to flourish in. I have noticed it before and it is simply not true. It is just that once or twice, as now, I have been drawn in at about the time when the seeds were planted, so naturally if a crisis follows, I know a lot more about what led up to it than the average outsider, who only hears about it after the event. Besides, I

18

don't believe you need to worry about Derek just yet. This is to be the full biography, you know, not merely one small bit of her life. From what my spies tell me, Pam and her family aren't the only pebbles on that beach; certainly not the only ones who'd like to stop publication, or indeed, better still, strangle the authoress before it gets to that point.'

'You mean she's been collecting up her dirty washing from all over the place?'

'Well, she would, wouldn't she, if that kind of thing amuses her? She must be around sixty after all and she's had an eventful life, one way and another. Oh, the lights are going down. We're off again.'

'Yes, and with all your chatter, I never got time to read the programme. Where are we now?'

'"Following Day. Morning Room of Lord Becher's house in Sussex." Where else?'

Clarrie did not occupy the star dressing room because, as was customary in plays of that period, the female protagonist was an elderly autocrat, who appeared in a succession of magnificent dresses and kept all the younger characters in their place by firing off cynical epigrams at the rate of two a minute.

She was played in the current revival by Dame Evadne Smythe, an octogenarian, with powerful lungs but unreliable memory and so arthritic that she was unable to sit down in any scene which later required her to stand up again. She was therefore loved and revered by the entire theatre-going public, whose members on this occasion chopped the play into small sections with rounds of applause to follow her every exit and every third epigram.

We could hear her booming away as we went past the open door of the number one dressing room and on to the next one, where Clarrie, in a pale blue cotton kimono, was removing her make-up under the rapt gaze of a farouche and tousled young man, dressed in a seaman's outfit which looked as though it had weathered many a North Sea gale.

The presence of only one admirer at this point in the day was well below par for the course, but he compensated for the numerical deficiency by occupying the whole of a couch made for three. One half was for himself and the other for a red and blue striped helmet and two bulging canvas knapsacks.

'Oh, come in, darlings! How lovely to see you both!' Clarrie trilled, not turning round, but speaking to our reflections. 'I'm nearly done. Have you met Steven? Tessa Crichton and Robin Price: Steven Westmore. Throw all that clutter on the floor, Stevie dear, so that Robin can sit where I can see him. You take that chair over there, Tessa darling. Now, tell me, what did you think? I want your absolutely honest, straight from the shoulder opinion and no hanky-panky.'

I responded to this in the accepted fashion by dishing out two minutes of unqualified praise, gallantly backed up by smiles and nods and unintelligible murmurs from Robin, but she still seemed hungry for more.

'Good! You are so marvellous, both of you, and I'm so glad you enjoyed yourselves. It went rather well for a matinee, didn't you think?'

'Super! They were hanging on every word.'

'And your seats were all right?'

'Perfect, thank you, Clarrie. Fifth row on the aisle, just what Robin likes.'

'I know, darling, I saw to it myself. It's a marvellous play, too, of course, isn't it? Awfully difficult to go wrong. Such heavenly construction, it practically plays itself. Don't you agree, Robin?'

Applied to directly on a subject he had clearly never given a moment's thought to, he found himself struggling a bit and I cast around for a means to extricate him. One way might have been to create a diversion by asking

Steven some leading questions about the joys and hazards of travelling in London on a motor bike, but I dismissed it, since his contribution to the conversation so far had been confined to yawns and grunts and it had not yet been established that he could speak English. Fastening on the single alternative that occurred to me, I said, 'And I'm told that the Seymour descendants are very strict about preserving the text, down to the last comma. Not a syllable to be altered or cut, is that right?'

'Oh yes, very true and quite right too, is what I say. Terrible things can happen when some clever director gets ideas about new interpretations.'

'And I can think of other terrible things that might happen if some directors I could name were told what to do and how to do it by the author's middle-aged daughter who'd never written a line of dialogue in her life.'

'Well, not yet, she hasn't, let's say,' Clarrie answered, turning round to wink at Steven.

'You refer to her ladyship's autobiography?'

'Oh, you've heard about that? You always know everything, don't you, Tessa? Tessa always knows everything, Stevie, so look out!'

Relieved now of the burden of having to bandy false words, Robin became articulate again.

'Have you time to step round the corner for a drink, Clarrie? I know you have to go on again in an hour, so maybe we should think about making a move.'

'Awfully sweet of you, darling, but I really believe the answer has to be no. I feel a little jaded, to tell you the honest, and it's such an effort to change twice over. I don't think Stevie feels much like it either, do you, darling? He's driven all the way down from Yorkshire or somewhere this morning, on his little machine, the intrepid fellow. If you want a drink, though, why don't we have one here? I'm sure there's a bottle or two in the cupboard.'

'Well, no, in that case,' Robin said, fazing me by getting

up and briskly putting an end to the discussion, 'let's make it some other time, shall we? Come on, Tessa, leave the poor girl to rest while she can.'

'Oh well, if you really have to dash... and thank you both from the bottom of my heart so very much for coming,' Clarrie said in an offhand voice, but with tears of gratitude glistening in her china-blue eyes, as she gazed up at him. 'It was so wonderful to see you and you've quite cheered me up with all the nice things you've said.'

'What was all that about?' I asked, when the two of us had stepped round the corner on our own.

'All what?'

'Hustling me out like that, as though you'd just noticed the theatre was on fire.'

'Well, it was practically forced on us, wasn't it? Anyone could see that she could hardly wait for us to leave. All she wanted was to be alone with the intrepid Stevie.'

'I realise that, but I wasn't going to let it worry me. I wanted to get a bit more out of her about Baba Seymour. That was the whole point of this boring expedition.'

'I don't know,' Robin said, putting on a big act of looking worried and concerned, 'can it be that you're slipping?'

'Yes, I suppose it can. In what way?'

'Didn't you notice all that grinning and giggling that went on when you brought the subject up?'

'Certainly, I did. Slipping I may be, but not blind and deaf. I could see that she'd got what's known as a meaningful relationship going at full tilt with that moron, but why should that bother me? Relationships come thick and fast in Clarrie's life, but the meaning is always exactly the same and two minutes' conversation with me wouldn't have taken any of the sparkle out of this one. All I was aiming for, when you cut me off in that peremptory way, was her views, plus any stray bits of gossip she may have picked up concerning Baba Seymour. The idea is to build up a picture of the adversary, so that we have a clear idea of what we're up against.'

'But you wouldn't have got it, you see. Or, if you had, the chances are that it would have been a false picture. That's what I meant about slipping. I'd have expected you to catch on as soon as I did, if not sooner.'

'Catch on to what? I do wish you'd explain.'

'Well, to be fair, I don't suppose you have any distinct memory of Pam, only having met her once, but the resemblance was quite startling.'

'Resemblance to what?'

'Steven, of course. His name was another clue and you certainly ought to have picked that one up because I remember Derek telling you that Baba had once been married to the Marquess of Doverfield and one of the facts I unearthed is that his eldest son is called Lord Westmore and the family seat is in Yorkshire.'

'Hang on a minute, Robin! You're not telling me that Stevie is Baba's son?'

'Why not? He has the right name, the right looks and he lives in the right county. What more do you want, quite apart from all the hysterical mirth from Clarrie? That's why I hauled you out of there, before you went plunging in up to your neck.'

'Yes, and I'm grateful. Clarrie wouldn't have spared me. Not that she's spiteful, but she has a peculiar sense of humour.'

'So rather a wasted afternoon, I'm afraid.'

'Oh, not entirely. The play had its moments, didn't you think? And, from the point of view of Derek and Pam, I am sure there must be something to be gained from it. Coincidences like that don't come our way for nothing, you may be sure. I must try and find some clever way to outwit little Miss Jones and somehow turn the situation to our advantage.'

Robin sighed. 'I honestly don't see the necessity. I've already explained that Derek was only letting off steam. He didn't seriously mean to involve you in his problems.'

'I know that, but it can't hurt anyone if I choose to involve myself. I've got over three weeks before rehearsals start, so I may as well use them that way as any other. I tell you what, Robin! Derek's not likely to be working tomorrow either, is he?'

'No.'

'So why don't we invite him and Pam to drive out to the country with us? If it's another hot day we could take a picnic and maybe call on Toby afterwards.'

'Oh, so Cousin Toby is to be drawn into the mesh now, is he?'

'Well, I should think he might be interested to meet a descendant of Kitty Lampeter. He's closer in age than we are to that period and Sheridan Seymour must have been the talk of the town when Toby was a lad. Besides, having become a playwright himself would give it an extra spice. Also he might be able to come up with some discreditable news about Baba, which could be used to blackmail her into changing her mind about publishing her memoirs.'

'I wouldn't be surprised and, with his devious mind and your insatiable curiosity working as a team, I don't give much for Baba's chances. Her days as an authoress must be numbered.'

THREE

Pam had gone to great lengths to ensure that her interesting condition did not pass unnoticed. She was dressed in a flowered smock which hung in folds from a high yoke and had entreated Robin to drive with extreme caution and at a funereal pace over the bumpy track across the Common to Toby's house.

Once there, she had declined to go into the pool, on the grounds that she would feel self-conscious in a bathing suit. Instead, she lay full length on a bamboo chaise-longue, with eyes closed, hands folded on her stomach, oblivious to everything, apparently, including her host, who was sitting a few feet away.

Toby was also a non-swimmer, although this had nothing to do with feeling self-conscious. It was simply that he was bone lazy and had no interest in any sport which did not allow for possibilities of cheating.

'Is she making rather too big a production of it,' I asked Robin, who had just completed his regulation ten lengths, 'or am I slipping again? I thought Derek told us the baby wasn't due until February?'

'There are extenuating circumstances, but you couldn't have known,' he replied, hauling himself up on to the tiled edge. 'I'd forgotten myself until Derek took me aside this morning and reminded me in a hushed voice.'

'Reminded you of what?'

'Pam had a miscarriage about six months ago. She was advised by the gynaecologist not to try again for at least a year, but of course the silly goose took no notice of that.

25

Now she's petrified that everything will go wrong again and it will end with her not being able to have children at all.'

'Any reason why it should?'

'Not that I know of, but she has a tendency to dramatise herself, as you've probably noticed. Derek thinks the form it's taking at present is for the purpose of building up her own confidence. Constantly drawing attention to the unborn helps to strengthen her belief that it's still there, in its right position and growing bigger and more beautiful by the minute. She seems to be one of those unfortunate people who've inherited a double share of the artistic temperament, without a drop of artistic talent to compensate.'

'Poor old Derek must have a hard time.'

'Oh, I don't think he sees himself in that light. She's the sun and moon and stars so far as he's concerned and he takes all her imaginary problems perfectly seriously, I regret to say.'

This was borne out by the scene now confronting us. Although Derek was working hard at splashing in and out of the water, his eyes rarely strayed from the supine figure on the chaise-longue and most of his exercise came from popping his head and shoulders over the rim of the pool to ask if she was feeling all right, not getting too much sun and wouldn't change her mind about coming in.

'And I daresay what really bothers you,' I suggested, after we had watched him go through this routine for the third or fourth time, 'is that if there should be any sort of domestic crisis arising from this blasted autobiography, it might have repercussions on Derek to the point where his work would suffer?'

'Which would be a pity because he's a bright boy, as well as conscientious and reliable, and he could have a long way to go.'

'So you ought to be grateful to me for trying to shut the

26

woman up, instead of nagging on about minding my own business.'

'That's because I know you so well. Once you get on the trail of something like this, you don't know where to stop. It can lead to no end of complications, mostly unpleasant and sometimes dangerous. There are more ways than one of being concerned about one's wife. Feel like another swim before we start making noises about leaving?'

'No, you go ahead while I change. I think the time has come to rescue Toby. You can tell from that drawn expression how badly Pam and Derek's antics are getting on his nerves, so I shall suggest that he and I take a little stroll across the Common.'

'Oh yes, extremely pretty,' Toby agreed, 'and also a crashing bore, which shouldn't come as any big surprise.'

'Why not?'

'Because her grandfather was a crashing bore too. Clever, but a snobbish, vain, conceited bore. He was also a moral coward.'

'You're a fine one to condemn him on that score!'

'Up to a point, perhaps, but Sheridan bombasted his way into situations which needed moral courage to sustain, whereas I have always gone to immense trouble to avoid them. There is a difference, you know.'

'If you say so, Toby. Pam takes after him in looks too, does she not?'

'I can't say I'd have noticed it if you hadn't told me who she was. I haven't thought about Sheridan Seymour for years, I'm thankful to say, but of course one can see a certain resemblance to Auntie Baba.'

'Oh, so you knew Baba too?'

'For a brief period. I seem to have met so many people, one way and another, on my journey through life, and usually to my cost.'

'How much did Baba cost you?'

'Very little, luckily. It was my wife who paid the price. My first wife, that is.'

Both Toby's wives had been detestable in their different ways, as he had discovered too late, but on the whole the first one, mercifully now deceased, had been marginally more detestable than the second.

'Tell me about it,' I said.

'It was when Baba got hold of the idea that she was destined for a great career on the stage. Nothing could have been more misguided, I must tell you. She had looks and what used to be called vivacity, but that was absolutely all. Even the Seymour cachet wasn't enough to trap any management into employing her. However, she was quite undaunted by that and it so happened that they were casting one of my plays at the time. Someone brought her down to one of those hideously boring and pretentious buffet luncheons which Irene liked to lay on. As soon as she entered the house it became obvious that she had no interest whatever in her escort. He had simply been used for the purpose of insinuating herself into what she mistakenly imagined to be my private circle of friends. As a matter of fact, I was scarcely on speaking terms with any of them. You were a lumpy adolescent in those days, but I daresay you remember those unspeakable people that social climbing Irene used to collect around her?'

'Vaguely, though I can't recall ever being invited to one of her parties. I take it that Baba's object was to charm you into speaking up for her to the casting director?'

'I expect so, but she wasn't a complete fool. Shrewd enough, anyhow, to recognise a lost cause when it was staring her in the face and she very smartly changed tactics and concentrated on Irene. She'd found a sitting duck there, you may be sure, specially as Baba was walking out with the earl of something or other at the time.'

'Although evidently not quite shrewd enough to per-

28

ceive that anyone who found favour with Irene automatically became persona non grata with you?'

'Evidently not. Not for some time, anyway.'

'Which is a pity, from my point of view. I'd been
hoping for a more up-to-date report.'

'Well, you will have to go to Ellen for that.'

'Why? What would Ellen know about it?'

'Something, I expect. Baba is her godmother.'

'Go on! You're joking, Toby?'

'Certainly not. Irene was about five months gone when
this historic meeting took place and when they became so
chummy one of Baba's gambits was to insist on being
godmother. I think she regretted it long before Ellen was
born, but she went through with it, after a fashion.'

'Ellen has never mentioned this to me.'

'Well, she wouldn't, would she? Baba sent her proxy
and a silver mug to the christening and I believe a string of
coral beads turned up on the first or second birthday, but
that was the last any of us heard from her for almost
twenty years.'

'And now?'

'Can't you guess? The thaw set in on the day that Ellen
announced her engagement to Jeremy, whose father, as
you may recall, not only has many millions tucked away
in the bank, but owns the bank that some of them are
tucked in. Within half an hour of Cinders walking down
the aisle on the arm of her Prince Moneybags she had
become Baba's favourite godchild.'

'And Ellen danced to her tune?'

'Not with a hop, skip and a jump, but you know Ellen.
She does her best to fob the woman off but she's too
good-natured to snub anyone, even the virtually unsnubb-
able. Besides, it would be a life's work to find excuses for
all the invitations which flow in. So she's obviously in a
better position than most to tell you about Baba's current
activities and machinations.'

29

'Specially being so observant, as well as good-natured. Thanks for the tip, Toby. I shall ring her up and suggest that the moment has come to extend the olive branch, with beads, bangles and baubles on it.'

On Monday morning, having telephoned Ellen and set some wheels turning in that quarter, I began my preparations for the third flank to make its advance into Seymour territory.

Ideally, this would have involved attiring myself in brogue shoes, ribbed woollen stockings and a shapeless tweed suit, which was inevitably what my hostess would be wearing, but, had I possessed such an outfit, the hot weather would have ruled it out, so I settled for dark blue linen, matching sandals and a discreet row of pearls.

The reason for this careful groundwork was that I was about to spend the day with my great-aunt Em, who lives in Gloucestershire and is very down on any form of ostentation. She has cause to be too, in a sense, because in recent days she has suffered quite a lot from it. Although Hamlet House, which has been her home since the day of her birth, is a plain, shabby not to say dilapidated building of no pretensions whatever, a surprising number of recent immigrants, whose houses had originally been constructed on the same lines, lived in the most flamboyant style, as was evinced by the fact that the Jaguars and Rolls-Royces which cluttered their drives could only have been there for decoration, since their owners never appeared to travel anywhere except on horses or by helicopter.

Furthermore, the undistinguished huddle of cottages, church and two pubs known as Little Pinbury was separated by only three miles from its infinitely more prosperous big sister, Great Pinbury. This contained such an abundance of thatched roofs, Cotswold stone, quaint cobblestones and Ye Olde Coaching Inns as to give the impression that it had been constructed to provide a setting for a breakfast food television commercial – a use, indeed, to which it was freqently put during those rare seasons when its roads were not lined with coaches and thronged with tourists surging in and out of the antique furniture and sheepskin leather shops.

I was aware that Aunt Em rarely set foot in this picturesque hurly-burly, preferring to do all her shopping at Norton-cum-Pinbury, which was four miles further away and quite an ugly place, with a very good Marks and Spencer. There was, however, one special address in Great Pinbury, which was the main objective of my expedition and, despite the objectionableness of its location, I knew I should face no opposition from Aunt Em in suggesting that after lunch we might take a look round it. This was because it had become her custom to spend the long winter evenings and even longer summer evenings watching television with one eye while the other guided her through some intricate and exquisite tapestry design, destined to adorn yet another Hepplewhite chair. Since it was also destined, no sooner in place, to be covered by a dirty old dustsheet, to protect it from the dogs' hairs, it was clearly the means more than the end which appealed to her. In fact, her appetite for the former had become more voracious with the passing years and her views on what constituted a worthwhile television programme corres-pondingly more flexible. She had reached the point where I believe she would not have considered moving out of Hamlet House if the roof had fallen in, destroying half the Hepplewhite chairs and one or two of the dogs as well, the reason being that Great Pinbury, in addition to more obvious claims to fame, was the headquarters of the British Needlework Association.

All this had been known for years by other members of Aunt Em's family besides myself. What I for one had not

32

realised until I started putting out enquiries about Baba and her siblings was that the present administrator and head saleswoman of the British Needlework Association was one Angela Petworth, *née* Seymour.

'I daresay you're old friends?' I remarked during lunch, which we ate in the kitchen, almost the only room in the house whose chairs were not draped in dustsheets.

'Me and Angie? Yes, we are.'

'Does she live in London and commute?'

'No, the only commuting she has to do is up and down the stairs. She lives over the shop. Very convenient.'

'Yes, it must be.'

'Means one can always rout her out and get her to open up after hours, if one happens to need something in a hurry,' Aunt Em explained, illustrating what she meant by convenient.

'No husband?'

'Not any more. There used to be one, but he died off, luckily.'

'What was lucky about it?'

'He was what they used to call a wastrel and a ne'er-do-well.'

'And do you know her sister, the one they call Baba?'

'Met her once or twice. Not with Angie, though. They're hardly on speaking terms.'

'Really? Why's that?'

'Couldn't tell you. Not my business, really. Shouldn't have thought it was yours, either, seeing that all you want from her is a simple little canvas and some wool, but you always were a terror for finding out things. You'd have used up your nine lives in your teens if you'd been born a cat. Got room for another baked apple?'

'Yes, please, and I do hope you've made it clear to her just how simple it's got to be? I'm an absolute beginner and I need something that a retarded child could do with its eyes shut.'

'Quite right! No good being too ambitious. You'd only make a mess of it and then lose heart and give up. Don't worry, I've explained it all to Angie and she'll have picked out a few which are just right for you. She can be a bit vague and woolly sometimes, but she'll probably rouse herself over this, as it's you.'

'Who has such an influential aunt, you mean?'

'Influential fiddlesticks! It was your name, not mine, which woke her up.'

'Oh, that's good! Is she a fan, by any chance?'

'Shouldn't think so, but she was born and brought up in your sort of world, you see. Her father wrote plays. Drawing room comedies, they used to be called. Very much in vogue when I was a girl, but of course people don't have time for that sort of twaddle nowadays.'

'You're wrong there, Auntie dear. One of his plays is being revived at this moment and you'd be surprised how many twaddle addicts are flocking to see it. Hadn't you heard?'

'No, I never go near London now and I don't read newspapers either. Too expensive, for one thing, and I get all the news and weather reports on television, which saves a lot of bother. What's this one called?'

'*A Woman of Low Repute.*'

'Oh, typical! Sheridan, as he called himself, was the most fearful snob. I'm surprised that anyone should want to go and see that sort of tosh in these enlightened days.'

'In fact, there are enough of them for the run to have been extended. Your friend, Angie, must be doing pretty well out of it.'

'Oh, I doubt that very much.'

'Why not? Rumours have reached me that she and her sisters made a very smart deal and are sharing out a percentage of the gross.'

'Then rumour, as usual, is most likely false. I don't understand the ins and outs of it, but the fact is that Angie

34

is one of those women who has never got her fair share of anything. She's what they call in the television plays one of life's losers.'

'Is she? I was also told that at the age of eighteen she married a very rich man and got a whacking great settlement from her father, as a reward for being such a good girl. But perhaps that wasn't true either?'

'Oh yes, true enough, as far as it went, but it wasn't very far. He only stayed rich for three or four years. By the time he died at the age of about forty, he'd run through all his own money and hers as well. That's why she has to have a job?'

'How did he lose it?'

'Oh, drink or gambling, I don't remember exactly, but it comes to the same thing.'

'I suppose so,' I admitted. 'When a man has been dead for nearly twenty years it wouldn't much matter to his widow whether he'd been a drunkard or a gambler. Still, there's an awful lot of money about in her family. Baba has seen to that and I imagine some of it is finding its way into Angie's bank account?'

Aunt Em frowned and shook her head at me, but when she spoke it was only to ask if I would be a dear and fetch her sewing bag from the morning room, as she might as well do something useful while we drank our coffee.

'Why do you look enigmatic and fob me off with harmless errands?' I asked on returning.

There followed a lot of heavy stage business of matching up bits of wool against the canvas, screwing up of eyes and pursing of lips while she threaded the needle, until at last she said, 'Knowing how one question can lead to another with you, I thought it might be wiser to leave the last one unanswered. However, I daresay there couldn't be any great harm in telling you. It's all so long ago now. Ancient history.'

'What was my last question? I've forgotten.'

'You asked me whether Angie would have benefited financially from this play of her father's and the answer is no.'

'Because of something that happened long ago and is now ancient history?'

'Quite so.'

'And therefore there would be no harm in my knowing about it?'

'There are two parts to the story, you see, and the first is quite simple and straightforward. When Sheridan died he left all his copyrights, or whatever they call them, equally between the three girls. A year or two later, when Angie's husband was still alive and she was so hard pressed for money, she sold her share outright to Baba for a thousand pounds. It seemed like a good bargain because there was no interest in the plays at that time and, apart from a trickle of fees from amateur companies, they weren't earning a penny. But Angie's a born loser, as I told you, and she ought to have realised at her age that anything Baba wanted to get her hands on would be worth having.'

'And, sure enough, the minute she'd parted with her share, it became a good investment again?'

'And do you know what Baba did then?'

'What?'

'Bullied or blackmailed or browbeat Dodie into parting with her share as well. Dodie's the eldest sister, they all have these silly nursery names, and she's a frightful coward and not very strong in the top storey. She's always been diabetic too, which has probably put her at a disadvantage. Anyway, there's Baba sitting on the lot and making sure, I wouldn't wonder, that not one penny finds its way to the other two.'

'What an odious woman she must be! On the other hand, I'd have thought that might make her easier to deal with.'

'Why?'

36

'Well, for instance, if they've no obligation and no need to feel squeamish or disloyal, why not take on Baba at her own game? A good lawyer might well be able to get the original terms of the will reinstated. At the very least, it would have the effect of bringing her shady dealings into the open and tarnishing her precious reputation, which might make her think twice. I see you don't agree?'

'I haven't said so.'

'But you're looking enigmatic again. Are you trying to dream up another little errand for me? Before you do, just tell me why you think Baba wouldn't mind being branded as a woman who cheated and robbed her own sisters?'

'The trouble is that, in my opinion, the question wouldn't arise. She has the whip hand, not only financially, but in other ways too.'

'What ways?'

'Oh, very well, I give in, but mind you keep this to yourself. It was Frances who told me. Nice woman – she was Sheridan's wife, you know, and she and I used to see a good bit of each other towards the end of her life. Her family used to live in these parts and when Sheridan died she moved into a little house on the estate. Nice woman, as I say; plain, but very friendly and unaffected. Angie's not unlike her, in some ways.'

'And what did Frances tell you?'

'She was badly worried. She asked me not to say a word about it to anyone and I never have until now. It was not that we were such close friends or anything, not in the same category as her great friend Kitty, for instance, but I think she felt this was something she couldn't possibly discuss with anyone in her family, or anyone who knew the girls, and she wanted some advice as to what she ought to do.'

'About what?'

'It was soon after Angie's husband died. A merciful release, if ever there was one. Frances came here one morning and told me that Baba had been down to see her the day before, in a great state. Very frightened and upset, or pretending to be.'

'It must have been pretence. I can't imagine her being frightened of anything.'

'Not for herself, for Angie. To cut a long story short, and it was a long one, she had reason to believe, proof in fact, that Angie had caused her husband's death by systematically dosing him with pills which hadn't been prescribed by his doctor. Come to think of it, I suppose he must have been an alcoholic, otherwise there'd have been more fuss about the death certificate.'

'And Baba told her mother she could prove this?'

'As far as I remember, her story was that she'd been tipped off by the nurse who'd looked after her brother-in-law during the last weeks of his life. Peter his name was, it's just come back to me. Anyway, as a result of that Baba had done a little quiet poking around on the afternoon of the funeral, when Angie was lying down. She'd found one bottle of pills among the medicines in the bathroom cupboard which had been dispensed by a chemist right over on the other side of London, Dulwich I think it was. She seemed to think this was damning enough and she may have been right, for all I know.'

'What did she do with the pills? Take them away to get them analysed?'

'I wouldn't put it past her, you know, Tessa, but she told Frances that she'd put them in her bag and later, when she'd got home, dumped them in the dustbin.'

'So that should have been enough, surely? What was left to be frightened about?'

'Well, according to Baba, she'd only done that to safeguard Angie, in case anyone else were to come across the pills and ask awkward questions. I don't know who she imagined would want to do that, but perhaps she was thinking of the nurse. Anyway, what she was afraid of, or pretended to be, was that when Angie came to herself and took in the full horror of what she'd done, she might fall into such a fit of remorse that she'd go haring off to Dulwich and collect some more pills to use on herself. It all sounded highly implausible to me, but Frances was incapable of believing that anyone could invent such a malicious tale and she swallowed it whole.'

'But you didn't?'

'No, but it wasn't up to me to disillusion the poor woman.'

'So what did you advise her to do?'

'Why nothing, of course. I said most likely the pills were perfectly harmless, some kind of vitamin rubbish which a friend had recommended and she didn't want her doctor to know she was taking them. In any case, I told her, whatever you do, not a word about it to Angie. I daresay Baba was dramatising a bit when she said the nurse had been dropping hints, or she imagined it, or it was just spite. Whatever the truth, I said, outside interference could only make matters worse. I can see now that it might have been bad advice.'

'Oh, why?'

'It might have been better to have got it all cleared up and put an end to then and there, because I have a shrewd idea that Baba didn't let it rest. I believe she was hoping her mother really would pass on a word of warning to Angie, but when that didn't happen she may have decided to pass it on herself. I'm only guessing, mind you, but the fact is that from about the time of Peter's death those two have scarcely been on speaking terms. I've sometimes wondered if that's why Angie buries herself down here and lives in such frugal style. It's almost as though she were going out of her way not to give Baba any cause for jealousy, like buying herself a new car, or some decent clothes once in a while. After all, she can't be so hard up as all that.'

'Why can't she?'

'Well, she earns quite a decent salary and her mother died ten or twelve years ago. She had pots of money, you know, and her family tied it up in such a way that Sheridan wouldn't be able to get his hands on the capital.'

'And she left it all to Angie?'

'Oh dear me, no. Frances couldn't have done anything like that, even if she'd wanted to. It was all in trust for the three girls, divided up equally between them. I suppose Baba was so rich herself by that time that it was a drop in the ocean to her, but Dodie seems to live quite comfortably on the income. Still, there it is. Nothing ever seems to have gone quite right for poor old Angie and you can lay your last penny on it that, if it ever came to a lawsuit, Baba would win hands down. She's got all the ammunition she needs and she wouldn't hesitate to use it, family or no family.'

'In that case, I have bad news for you. I have a feeling that she may be about to use it anyway,' I said and proceeded to give an up-to-date account of work in progress on the autobiography.

FIVE

'It worked!' Ellen said, greeting me at the front door. 'I cast a spell to make you come punctually and you have!'

'On the early side, if anything. I was hoping to get ten minutes with you, in camera, before your other guest arrived.'

'You did right and, luckily, Baba doesn't know the meaning of time, so we might be able to stretch it to half an hour. Let's sit down and have a drink while you tell me the news. I hear you and Robin were at Roakes, visiting my dad the other day.'

She led the way into her somewhat palatial drawing room, which was saved by the skin of its teeth from being oppressively luxurious by an element of sweet disorder. Books and newspapers were strewn about in a haphazard way and the telephone had been left on the floor, alongside an open address book, indicating that the room was used for living in and not just kept in readiness for the magazine photographers.

'Yes, we were,' I said, 'and this is turning out to be quite a week for visiting relatives. I had lunch with Aunt Em yesterday. She took me over to Pinbury to see a friend of hers called Angie Petworth, who runs a needlework shop.'

'Well, she would, I suppose. It's hard to imagine Aunt Em having many friends who didn't.'

'This one is special, though, because as well as being Aunt Em's friend, she is Baba's sister. Have you met her?'

'No, I don't think so. I did meet one sister a few months ago, when Baba roped us both in to address envelopes for one of her charities, but her name wasn't Angie.'

'Dodie, I expect. What's she like? Attractive-ugly, with a large nose, beautiful hands, very thin and a drawly voice?'

'No, nothing at all like that. Why would you think so?'

'It was a thumbnail sketch of Angie. I think she must take after her mother, who was reputed to have been plain, but good-natured and loaded with charm. How about Baba? I know what she looks like because one is always seeing photographs of her and she's obviously a female version of Sheridan Seymour, but how does she rate on charm?'

'Loads of it too, when it suits her. She'll probably go all out on you and, come to think of it, she may not be late today, after all. She's agog to meet you.'

'Is she really? I must admit I find that endearing.'

'It's probably a sign that you're moving into the big time. She has a nose for that sort of thing.'

'Then let's hope it's picked up the right scent and not mixed me up with someone else. Does she ever talk to you about her book?'

'Does she not? The hard part is getting her to stop.'

'But you haven't been allowed to read it?'

'No one has, as far as I can make out. To tell you the truth, I don't believe there's a lot actually written yet and I doubt if there ever will be.'

'Why not?'

'Well, see what you think when you meet her,' Ellen said, getting up to replace the telephone on its table as the doorbell rang.

'I think I may have met your son the other day,' I said at lunch, which had been jigging merrily along to Baba's tune. She was one of those unsatisfactory people whom it is easier to dislike in theory than in practice. Despite almost every word she uttered betraying her as ignorant, snobbish or conceited, if not all three at once, it was

42

delivered with so much artless exuberance as often to make it more endearing than offensive, thus undermining my sternest efforts to loathe and despise her.

She had told me several times what a thrill it was to meet me and at least twice that I was one of the few young actresses in London who was clearly audible in the back row of the theatre, though not revealing by what accident she had discovered this.

'I think I must have too,' I added, 'because I can see now that he looks awfully like you.'

This was true because, despite a thickening of the jaw and waistline, it was easy to see that in her youth she had been the original model from which both Steven and Pam had been copied, although in her case there was an excess of vitality which would have been all the better for having been parcelled out between the three of them.

'I have two sons,' she said, 'and I am deeply flattered to hear that I look like either of them. They are easily the most tiresome, spoilt and selfish boys God ever put breath into, but, at the risk of sounding like a besotted mother, which is one thing I am most definitely not, I have to say that they really are rather gorgeous looking. Did I tell you, Ellen, that dear old Dan Erskine spent a whole morning last week photographing Steven?'

'Yes, I believe you did mention it.'

'And what's more, he insisted on traipsing all the way up to Yorkshire to do it. He said it was so terribly important to set Stevie in his true ambience and environment. I must admit I was rather impressed when they told me. When I was about Stevie's age and Dan did some absolutely stunning photographs of me, I can never tell you how flattering, I had to trudge all the way over to his studio in Fulham, or somewhere ghastly. He always made an absolute rule about it. No exceptions at all, not even the Royals, so I'm told.'

'Yes, that's right,' I said in the pause for breath which

followed these reminiscences, 'Steven was the one I met.'

'Well, I suppose it would have been, really. Perry, Steven's half-brother, is abroad at present, staying with some multi-millionaires in California. The daughter is a friend of his, an absolute poppet and couldn't be more beautiful, she was educated partly in England. The father owns about twenty-five factories which turn out millions of gallons per minute of some revolting fizzy drink, I can't remember what it's called. He wants Perry to become his Vice-President, which sounds fearfully grand, although I'm sure it isn't really, but I think it's quite shrewd of the old boy to be so keen to take him into the fold. My odious son is frightfully apt to put on a big act of being the world's biggest nitwit and not everyone realises he can be quite bright when he wants to. Now he rings up about four times a day to ask my advice, if you please, about whether he should accept or not. "How would I know?" I tell him, and "Isn't it about time you made up your own mind and let go of the apron strings?" Where did you meet Steven?'

'In Clarrie Jones' dressing room. Robin and I went round to see her after the show.'

'Oh, you've seen the play, have you? How marvellous! Do tell me what you thought of it, I can't wait to hear the professional verdict. Sheridan Seymour was my father, you know, but you needn't let that worry you. I shan't be in the least offended if you tell me you were bored to tears.'

'I wasn't. It's a marvellous play. So beautifully constructed.'

'Ah, there speaks the true pro! She's absolutely right, you know, Ellen. The general public, bless their little cheque-books, haven't the remotest understanding about that sort of thing, but I have yet to meet an actor who wasn't overboard about Papa's plays, from the construction point of view.'

44

'Including Clarrie,' I said. 'You know her, of course?'

'Oh yes, peculiar young woman in some ways, isn't she? I must be very careful what I say here, I know that, but do tell me what she's really like underneath all the affectation.'

'Exactly like she is on top. She's one of the few people of my acquaintance who doesn't bother to put on an act.'

'Oh, God, really? I can't tell you how you're depressing me.'

'Have a tiny bit more *crème chocolat*?' Ellen suggested in a soothing voice.

'No, I really mustn't, thank you, darling. It's simply delicious, but I have to be ultra careful about my blood pressure.'

'Oh dear, is chocolate bad for that? I hadn't realised.'

'Never mind, but I have to stick to an absolutely rigid diet. . . . Oh, I don't know, though. Perhaps I can't resist one tiny spoonful, if you're both going to.'

'Good! How has Tessa depressed you?'

'Well, you see, girls, in strictest confidence, I've been working so hard at trying to convince myself that Clarrie wasn't serious about my poor Stevie. I told myself it was a little game she was playing because it amused her to have him around. One could understand that. Quite a feather in her funny little cap really, because, ghastly as he is, even I have to admit that he is rather beautiful, quite apart from the title and so on, which would be another attraction, I daresay. All quite harmless, I told myself, and probably do him a power of good to have a little frolic with a woman so much older and more experienced than himself. I am afraid what Tessa, with the kindest intentions in the world, no doubt, has done is to confirm that nagging fear at the back of my mind that Clarrie means business. I have a nasty feeling that she is hoping to marry him.'

'I daresay she is,' I agreed. 'Her intentions always start by being honourable, but I don't think you have anything

45

to worry about. Luckily, there is an insuperable impediment to her marrying anyone just at present.'

'And what is that, may one ask?'

'She may have forgotten to mention this, but she has a husband already.'

'But, my dearest Tessa, can't you see how that makes the situation worse than ever?'

'I can see how you might feel it would. You have visions of your boy being dragged through the divorce courts and pilloried by the press, to quote a line from your father's play, but believe me, Lady Doverfield, there is very little danger of it. The run will have ended long before things come to that pass and Clarrie will have moved on to pastures new. If she remembers Steven at all, it will only be as just another jolly little episode in her fun-filled life.'

There is no pleasing some people, however, and Baba did not look particularly relieved to hear her loathsome angel described in these terms. In fact, her expression made it plain that I had totally misjudged the situation, so I put my case to arbitration.

'Isn't that right, Ellen?'

'Oh yes, I'm sure it is. You always know everything about everyone and you're such a good judge of character. You always liked Jeremy from the beginning, even when Dad was being so hellish about him, and you've been friends with Clarrie for ages. I'd forget about it if I were you, Baba, and concentrate on counting your blessings.'

'What blessings, I should like to know?'

'Just remember all the lovely money you're making out of the play and now getting the run extended and everything. You must admit it's mainly thanks to Clarrie.'

'Not at all. She's competent enough, I grant you, and I suppose she looks attractive, in her blowzy way, but there are dozens of young actresses who could do the part just as well. Tessa, to name but one. As she's just pointed out, the part is so brilliantly written, with so many funny lines, that it would be impossible to go wrong.'

Besides being a backhanded compliment and misquotation, this was pure claptrap and I was about to bounce back into the fray when I saw Ellen wrinkling her nose at me, signifying that I should restrain myself.

'Okay, then,' she said, 'so you'll be able to get your own back by putting all that in your book. How's it going, by the way?'

'Terribly, terribly, wonderfully well. It has taken me all these years to discover that I am literally one of those born writers. I just go on and on, the only thing that holds me up is lack of time, and I've had the most fantastic stroke of luck. Didn't I tell you? You're always so interested that I felt sure I must have and I don't want to repeat myself.'

'Well, I do seem to remember your hinting something, but I don't know any of the details,' Ellen said, casting another warning glance in my direction. 'What's happened? Have you had an offer for the American rights?'

'Oh yes, dozens, as it happens, but we haven't decided which one to take up yet. My publishers seem to think we might do better to wait until it comes out over here before committing ourselves and naturally I leave all that boring business side to them. That's their job, after all. I just have to chug along and do all the creative part. Not that I'm complaining because I do find it the most tremendous fun and the words simply pour out. Getting them into the right order is rather more of a chore, but I can say in all modesty that I'm beginning to master it now.'

'So what about this wonderful stroke of luck?'

'It came out of the blue about a month ago and I'm rather surprised you haven't heard about it because some enterprising journalist got hold of the bones of the story, God knows how, and wrote it up in one of the evening papers. Still, I mustn't imagine that the whole world is thirsting for knowledge about my humble little book. Tessa doesn't look bored, which is encouraging, but then one can never be sure with actresses.'

'Tessa is not at all bored,' Ellen said firmly. 'She'd love to hear about it and so would I. What happened a month ago?'

'Very well, if you insist on dragging it out of me, I had a letter from a young woman using a box number address in Chelmsford. Or it might have been Chingford. Never mind, that doesn't matter. The important thing was that she told me she had just moved into a new house which had been left to her by an aunt, who had died in a nursing home. One day when she was clearing out the attic, she had come across a battered old trunk and inside was a bundle of letters, which she had found fascinating reading. By some extraordinary fluke, she'd just read the newspaper story about how I was writing my family memoirs and she thought I might be interested in these letters.'

With this announcement the significance of Ellen's sign language finally dawned on me and, if Baba had been gratified before, she might well have been overwhelmed by the attentive expression I could have turned on her now, had not caution toned it down a little.

'How absolutely riveting and romantic,' I said politely. 'Just like the opening of a Henry James story.'

'Yes, how right you are! Exactly the same thought occurred to me and the marvellous part was that it all lived up to its promise. They were letters which had been written by my father to this girl's aunt, Elizabeth her name was, when he was in his fifties and she was about eighteen. At least, that's when they started, but the correspondence went on for several years.'

'Love letters?'

'In the truest and most romantic sense. She obviously adored him, but it's equally plain from the tone of his letters that their love was never consummated, as they say.

48

That must sound incredible to your generation, but it didn't to me. My father was far too upright and honourable a man to have seduced a girl of less than half his age, however much she may have invited it. Their meetings seem to have been confined to occasions like tea at the Ritz and strolling in Kensington Gardens. All very pure and unsullied. Heaven only knows what all my younger readers are going to make of it.'

'You've actually read these letters? You asked to and she sent them?'

'Well, no, it wasn't quite as simple as that, naturally. I shall have them eventually, with full authority to publish whatever excerpts I choose, but people seem to know the value of everything these days and of course one can't deny that they would fetch a fortune in the open market. It may take a little while for my lawyers to beat her down to a reasonable price. That's their idea, at any rate, although I don't intend to let the expense stand in my way. I mean to get my hands on them, however much it costs.'

'Quite right,' Ellen agreed in the indulgent tone she seemed to reserve for her godmother, 'they will make a nice little chapter for your book. Always provided they're genuine, of course.'

'Oh, they're genuine all right. I haven't seen the originals yet, but this woman sent me photographed copies of a selection of them, a sort of sample package, and I was able to compare the writing with some letters I had from him myself at about that time. There's simply no question at all about their authenticity and they're going to provide a lot more than one chapter, that I can promise you. He seems literally to have poured out the secrets of his heart to this Elizabeth and told her the most intimate details of his life. She must have had an exceptional character for him to have confided in her so freely, although I imagine her being so far removed from his own world and the fact that they so rarely met in public may

49

have had a liberating effect too.'

'What sort of intimate details?' I enquired. 'I suppose it's permissible to ask, since you propose to publish them anyway?'

'Well, for instance, and this is by far the most extraordinary and amazing of the lot, has either of you ever heard of an actress called Kitty Lampeter? I don't suppose Ellen has, but you might, Tessa?'

'Oh me, too,' Ellen said, jumping in again before I could answer, 'my dad fell madly in love with her when he was fourteen and he's got a whole collection of tinted photographs of her looking soulful and ethereal.'

'Then she must have engaged a very brilliant photographer because those are the last words to describe her. She was the biggest whore in London and greedy, ill bred and deceitful as well.'

'Is that how he described her to Elizabeth?' I asked.

'Not in those words, naturally. He was the most chivalrous man on earth, where women were concerned, but one can read between the lines and draw one's own conclusions.'

'I call that very clever,' Ellen said without a smile, 'I am sure I could never have drawn that conclusion if he was really so chivalrous.'

'What I mean is, my darling girl, he didn't condemn her, but her behaviour speaks for itself. It is quite clear that my father did have some kind of an affair with her. I'm not denying that because he confessed as much to Elizabeth, but the infatuation, or whatever it was, must have worn off very quickly, after only a few months, in fact. Or, to be precise, it did for him. Miss Lampeter had other ideas.'

We both looked dutifully expectant and she went on:

'Some months after they parted she wrote and asked him to call on her, as she had a business matter she wished to discuss with him. He had always thought of her as a good-natured, artless sort of woman and he had no compunction about obeying the summons. He assumed she wanted his advice about her lease, or something of that sort. In some ways, you know, girls, I think she must have had a lot in common with Clarrie. That's why, despite what Tessa assures me, I have these hideous forebodings about my poor boy falling into the same kind of trap.'

'Why?' Ellen asked. 'What sort of hideous trap did your father fall into?'

'It came near to ruining his life. When he arrived at her flat that afternoon Kitty told him she was going to have his child. There was no way he could prove she was lying. It could have been his and, needless to say, she had left it far too late for an abortion. Being the sort of man he was, he agreed to stand by her. He would accept paternity and pay for the confinement in a private nursing home and thereafter give her a monthly allowance. However, he made it plain that he never wished to set eyes on the child and that all correspondence was to be conducted through his solicitors.'

'Which should have been the end of the story,' I remarked, 'but I have the impression there was more to come?'

'A great deal more, the persecution was only just beginning. Perhaps you'd care to hear how she later had two more children and managed to palm them both off as his?'

'We're dying to,' Ellen assured her, 'because it must have taken a bit of doing, if he'd given up seeing her – but oughtn't you to save it for your book?'

Baba appeared to give serious consideration to this question, but the right answer soon occurred to her.

'Yes, I do see what you mean, Ellen. One does have to be so careful, as a rule, but I know how wonderfully discreet you are and I feel sure Tessa is too. I have an instinct about people in that way and it's always absolutely right. Also, speaking now as a writer, I feel it would be

51

useful to give you what we call a rough draft of the final version. It could help a lot when it came to the actual writing. And it's going to be such an important part of the book that it would be really valuable to test it out on two intelligent people like yourselves and get your reactions.'

'Oh well, if you feel we could be a help to you, no more argument. Do go ahead!'

'And you do promise not to pass it on? No, no, of course you wouldn't and it was so shrewd of Tessa to guess that the story hadn't ended, although my poor papa was in no way to blame for that. It was Kitty Lampeter who realised what a cushy life she could make for herself, if she played her cards right and she was a very clever and cunning woman. Really, one could almost admire her utter brazenness, if it wasn't all so distasteful. You'll simply never guess what she did when it sank in that she wouldn't get any more out of my father by straightforward means.'

'No, we couldn't possibly. What did she do?'

'The most impudent thing you could imagine from a woman in her situation. She went to see my mother and took the baby with her. It was a very pretty child, which probably helped, because my poor mama was so sweet and sentimental by nature, although not terribly bright, unfortunately. Absolutely any charlatan could get round her. My father used to say that if she came home and found burglars ransacking the house they'd only to tell her that their children were starving and she'd have helped them pack up the silver and offered them a cup of tea before they left.'

'And what did she offer Kitty? Money, presumably?'

'Oh yes, indeed, all she wanted, but that was only the beginning. Naturally, Kitty spun the tale about being so hard up and how she couldn't take jobs in the theatre unless she had the child adopted and she'd rather starve and so on and so on. And, naturally, my mother fell for it.

She undertook to arrange for the allowance to be doubled and said there was absolutely no reason for Kitty to hide herself away like a criminal. She must bring the baby round whenever she felt like it. It could go into the nursery and play with her own children, so that Kitty could take an afternoon off sometimes, to do some shopping and meet her friends.'

'What a lovely woman she must have been, your mother. I've often heard people say how good she was,' I remarked.

'Oh yes, she was kind and generous, but so terribly unworldly, I'm afraid all sorts of people took advantage of her. Kitty was quite shameless. She used to dump her wretched offspring on us, Rita its name was, three or four times a week, even before she went back on the stage. When our poor old Nanny complained about it and threatened to give notice, my mother simply hired an extra nursery maid to help her out. Rita was virtually brought up as one of the family.'

'And how did your father feel about this arrangement?'

'Furious and resentful, of course, but we didn't know anything about that at the time. It wasn't until years later that we learnt the sordid truth and I suppose the fact is that he was powerless to do anything about it. He'd accepted responsibility for the beastly brat and, so far as my mother was concerned, that was that. She couldn't be made to see why it should be treated differently from all his other children. Would you like to hear how Kitty repaid her, repaid them both?'

It was tempting to ask whether she had done so by writing a book about them, but, taking my cue from Ellen's dead-pan expression, I restrained myself and Baba answered her own question:

'By foisting a couple more bastards on them. God knows who the father or fathers may have been, but she let it be assumed that they came from the same stable as the first one. I don't know whether even my gullible mother believed this, but she never questioned it openly and since by then Kitty had become more or less a fixture in our household the legend grew up that her position there was what you might call resident concubine. Not a very nice situation for my sisters and me to have to live with when we were old enough to understand it.'

'No, horrid, but all the same might it not have been true?' Ellen suggested. 'I've heard of women who take that line when they realise their husbands are being unfaithful to them. They prefer his infidelities to be confined to the one devil they do know, instead of nameless devils outside their control.'

'Oh, I daresay there are such women, but my mother wasn't one of them. Everyone said she was a saint, but, if so, she was like a good many other saints. All the time and money in the world for the undeserving beggars and sinners, but her own family could go to the wall. And Kitty wasn't the only one who made a good thing out of it, I might tell you. Every one of her progeny has been trading on the Seymour name since early childhood. We never resented it so much with Rita. She was easily the best of the bunch and I daresay she had a right to flaunt her illegitimacy, if she wanted to, but the other two hadn't even that much to boast about. I doubt if either of them ever set eyes on their real father, or knew what his name was. As for Laura, everyone knows she wouldn't have managed to get a publisher to consider one of her fifth-rate books if it hadn't been cleverly put around that she was our half-sister.'

'I haven't met Laura,' I admitted, 'but I've seen photographs of her and of your father too, of course, and the resemblance is quite striking.'

'I am well aware of that, my dear, but perhaps, unlike Ellen, you have never seen photographs of Kitty Lampeter? She happens to have been beautiful in her way and remarkably well bred looking, considering her background. She was also very much the same type and colouring as my father. They could almost have been brother and sister.'

'Yes, I suppose that's true. I hadn't thought of it.'

'It's what made it so easy to pass her three children off as our cousins, which is how they were explained away to us when we were small. Anyway, that game's up now. I've got it in writing, in Papa's own, unmistakable hand, or soon will have, that he had lost all interest in Kitty even before Rita was born and that the two younger children were nothing whatever to do with him. It's all down in black and white in a letter to Elizabeth which this woman has sent me and she assures me that there are numerous references to the subject throughout the correspondence. That's why she thought I might want to use it to clear his name, which is exactly what I intend to do. It's the chance I've been waiting for all my life and, now it's come, I'm going to show up every one of those Lampeters for the lying frauds they are.'

SIX

'There was simply no arguing with her,' I told Robin that evening. 'Ellen tried, in her tactful way, to point out that she might do herself more harm than good by dragging out all the old scandals, but Baba wouldn't listen. Revenge has become her obsession, although she doesn't call it by that name. Vindication is her word for it and nothing will budge her. It's terrifying to realise what jealousies and resentments she's been building up all these years.'

'No wonder she has high blood pressure! Did you manage to find out any more about the anonymous woman in Chingford or Chelmsford, who so fortuitously came across this bundle of letters?'

'No, and that was odd too, in its way. She talks non-stop and pours out the most fearful indiscretions and defamatory remarks, which appear to be spontaneous, but she can be cagey too, at times. Ellen tried her out on that one, but she couldn't get the woman's surname out of her, or the name of the people who'd owned the house before. Do you suppose she made the whole thing up?'

'She wouldn't go as far as that, surely? What would be the point?'

'I can't imagine, but I wouldn't put it past her. I'd say she was capable of going to any lengths to get what she wanted and she's so puffed up with her own magnificence that it would simply never occur to her that she might come a cropper.'

'Maybe not, but it would certainly occur to a lawyer. He must have warned her about the chances of the Lampeter side suing when the book came out and that

56

they'd almost certainly win their case, with huge damages, unless she could prove the letters were genuine and could name their source. That wouldn't be much of a revenge.'

'I'm not sure that you've quite got her measure, Robin. If she's as arrogant and conceited as I suspect, lawyers wouldn't come into it. She'd have invented them as well, to fend off awkward questions.'

'Then she must be an even bigger fool than you took her for. How could she imagine that any reputable publisher would print such dangerous material without at least making sure that it was authentic?'

'Then perhaps hers are not reputable and I presume there would be one or two of the other kind who would accept her word for it? She is, after all, a well known character, besides being rich, titled and the daughter of a celebrated man.'

'Not to mention well skilled in forgery, presumably? Or do you suspect that these letters don't exist at all, even in some spurious form?'

'How can one tell? Neither Ellen nor I could make up our minds on that point. In the end, though, we came to the conclusion that she wouldn't take such an enormous risk as that and therefore that it was a toss-up.'

'Between what?'

'Well, first of all there's a remote chance that what she told us was true. The letters do exist and were written by Sheridan to put himself in a good light with some romantic girl whose ardour had begun to cool with the discovery that her hero was reputed to be keeping a mistress under his wife's roof. He was an intensely vain man and admiration from any quarter was the breath of life to him, so it's a possibility which has to be taken into account. What gives one pause, though, is that the one thing that Baba had been praying for all her life should have dropped into her lap, without any effort on her part, just when she needed it most and could make the best use

57

of it. Don't you find that a bit hard to swallow?'

'What's the alternative?'

'The one we prefer is that she hired herself an accomplice.'

'Who lives, for the sake of argument, in Chingford or Chelmsford?'

'Exactly! And that's why she won't be pinned down.'

'But could she really find anyone who would lend themselves to a fraud of that kind, specially since it would be such an easy one to expose?'

'Maybe, if the money was tempting enough, and there can be no doubt that in a situation like this expense would be no object. On the other hand, we also have to remember that Baba was not above resorting to a little blackmail on at least one occasion.'

'Is that a reference to the story Aunt Em told you?'

'Yes, it is and, if she could do such a thing to her own sister, I can't see anything to stop her trying it on with someone else. The annoying part is that there doesn't seem to be any way to scare her off. If she's determined to go ahead, no threats or persuasions will stop her. And, if it should end with a libel action and she were to lose it, I still can't see how that would help our lot. In fact, it could make things worse than ever. There'd most likely be a backlash of sympathy for Baba and people would say no smoke without fire and all that twaddle. So, instead of the book being read by a handful of people who lap up anything which hints at scandal in high places, every coffee-table owner in the land would be queueing up for it. And it's not much use hanging around and hoping she'll drop dead before the beastly book is finished.'

'Although I don't see much else you can do.'

'Neither do I at the moment. Judging by the way she gobbled up her lunch today, she ought to have died years ago from over-eating, but she's obviously got the constitution of a camel. Still, at least it's not a mad rush against time. Ellen takes the attitude that there's a lot more

58

talking about the book going on than actual writing of it and she knows Baba of old, so she may well be right. It could be months before we reach the crisis.'

Robin did not look particularly relieved to hear this and he said, 'Which I take to mean that you're not ready to admit defeat just yet? May one ask what further pranks you have in mind?'

'Well, as it happens, there is just one promising source which has still to be tapped.'

'Which is?'

'It's called Dodie, short for Dorothy. She's the eldest of the three Seymour sisters and apparently she's been bullied and imposed on by Baba ever since they were tots. It might not be a bad idea to find out a little more about her.'

'And how do you propose to do that? Ring her up and invite her to tea?'

'Not me, no, but Ellen's met her once or twice and she and I are hatching another little plot.'

'You've certainly succeeded in pulling Ellen into this maelstrom. Have you been doing a bit of bullying yourself?'

'I wouldn't dream of such a thing. Red hot irons wouldn't persuade Ellen to do anything against her better judgement. I simply explained the situation to her and she was all for doing what we could to help. She has no particular feeling for or against Baba and she's never met a Lampeter in her life, but she's always on the side of the lame dog, as you know so well.'

'And there seem to be a few in need of a leg up here, but what exactly are you hoping to get from Dodie?'

'That remains to be seen. We shall have to write the script as we go along. It did cross our minds, though, that Dodie might recently have acquired a little property in Chingford or Chelmsford.'

'Wherein to practise the arts and skills of calligraphy?'

'Something like that, yes.'

* * *

'Sorry, Tess, nothing doing,' Ellen said the next morning, when I telephoned her for a progress report.

'Never mind, I'm sure you tried your best.'

'Yes, and it's disappointing because I had such a lovely excuse lined up for her. I was going to say that Jeremy's mother was scouring the country for someone really competent to help out with her charity work and could she see her way to obliging? It would have been absolutely true too, that was the beauty of it. My mother-in-law is permanently racked by guilt about being so disgustingly rich and she feels she can only justify keeping a butler and chef and at least two chauffeurs by tearing about non-stop from one committee meeting to the next. So she's always on the look-out for willing hands to take on some of the donkey work.'

'I suppose she might justify it equally well by shelling out some of the wages to her charities and doing a bit of driving and cooking herself?'

'Except that's not how people's husbands get life peerages, as you probably know.'

'So what went wrong with your lovely story?'

'She wasn't there to hear it. After you left here yesterday I tried about four times to telephone her, but there was never any reply, so I thought I'd leave it for a bit. When I tried again this morning it was answered by the woman who lives in the flat next door. It was just a fluke really. She'd come in because she'd seen the milk left outside yesterday morning and she thought Dodie might be ill or something. Apparently they have a mutual arrangement about that sort of thing.'

'And what did she tell you?'

'That Dodie wasn't there and her bed hadn't been slept in. She sounded a bit put out because Dodie hadn't given her any warning and she hadn't the faintest idea where she'd gone, or when she'd be back. I gather it wasn't particularly unusual, though. This neighbour, whoever she was, went moaning on for about five minutes about how vague and absent-minded Dodie was.'

'I'm sorry you got let in for all that, Ellen, but on the whole I see it as rather good news.'

'What a relief! I thought you'd be disappointed.'

'Well, it's a nuisance, I admit, in so far as it gums up the immediate plan, but it must be only a postponement, don't you think? She can't stay away for ever without letting it be known where she's gone. And, in the meantime, I see this mysterious disappearance as highly significant. I bet you all the money Jeremy's got in the bank that there's one person who knows exactly where she is and how to reach her.'

'You mean Baba?'

'And you see what that implies?'

'Not exactly. No, not at all.'

'Baba has got the wind up and removed a potentially damaging witness out of our reach.'

'Honestly, Tess, I think you over-estimate her. She's not nearly sharp enough to have seen through our wide-eyed act, or suspected us of having an ulterior motive for encouraging her to babble on as we did.'

'Okay, let's say that she didn't catch on at the time, but she did realise when she got home that she might have babbled on a bit too freely and so now she's trying to undo some of the mischief. Whichever way it was, it must now be fair to assume that there's something bogus about the lady from Chelmsford or the other place.'

'You may be right, but isn't it equally fair to assume that, if she's gone to the bother of sending her poor sister into hiding, we're unlikely to find out what her game is?'

'Oh well, as I said, it's probably only a temporary set-back. Dodie is bound to surface sooner or later, unless of course Baba has imprisoned her in that mysterious old attic under a pile of sacks, in which case there's nothing we can do about it and we shall have to cast our nets elsewhere.'

'Where would that be?'

'Another trip to Pinbury, I should imagine, and tomorrow would be the very day for it.'

'Why tomorrow?'

'Because it's the first Thursday of the month. Feel like coming?'

'Not tomorrow, Tessa. I've got to do some important shopping and then pack my bags. Friday is our wedding anniversary and we're going to Paris for a long weekend. Awfully sorry?'

'Don't be. I can't expect you to disrupt your life just to please me.'

'You seem to be disrupting yours, though.'

'Oh, that's different. The outcome of this affair affects Robin ultimately and, anyway, if I weren't doing this, I shouldn't be shopping and packing for a weekend in Paris. I should be sitting at home, thinking I ought to be learning my lines, or turning out my wardrobe, which would be infinitely more tedious. . . .'

'Yes, I'm beginning to get the hang of it now,' I told Aunt Em when I rang up half an hour later. 'In fact, at this rate I'll have finished by the end of the week. I think I'm ready for something more ambitious and I wondered if your Associated Lady would be there, if I were to come down tomorrow.'

'Bound to be. Sorry I can't give you lunch, though. Tomorrow's my day for the WI and I shall be over at Norton.'

'Oh yes, so you will, what a shame! Never mind, I'll bring the canvas down to show you when it's finished, so long as you promise not to be too critical.'

'Want me to ring Angie and ask her to put out a few more for you to look at?'

'Oh, that'd be kind. And tell her I'll aim to get there by twelve, will you?'

'Try not to be later. Thursday's early closing day.'

'Right! Thanks awfully, Aunt Em, and have a great time with the Women's Institute.'

'Should be interesting. They've got a guest speaker coming down to give us a talk on "Tapestry through the Ages".'

SEVEN

I was fifteen minutes late for the appointment and Angie was running the shop on her own. She explained that, as Thursday was early closing day and always a slack one for business, she usually allowed her two assistants to leave early.

She appeared to be in no hurry to do so herself, however, and showed not a trace of impatience when, having whittled the canvases of my choice down to three, I was still unable to decide between them.

At one point she ambled away to lock the door and switch the sign round from Open to Closed, but on returning made no reference to this, reverting to the theme of pros and cons, as though she had all the time in the world to put at my disposal.

No two women could have been less alike than she and Baba and, had I not known better, I would not have believed they could be related at all. Even more striking than the difference in colouring and features was the contrast of personality. Where Baba's words came clattering out and tumbling over each other, practically every one centring on herself, Angie personified detachment and laconicism and her speech was so slow and drawly that in the time it took her to complete one sentence Baba could have rattled off half a dozen.

'Oh dear, I do apologise,' I said, looking at the card, 'I hadn't realised we'd gone past closing time.'

'Doesn't matter. Shut for the day now, so take your time.'

'Well, why not come round the corner and have lunch

with me? I'd really appreciate it because I hate eating alone and I shouldn't have to feel so guilty about taking so long to make up my mind.'

Angie had a trick of looking as though she found the most ordinary remark faintly comical and she used it now.

'Better idea. Come up to the flat and I'll find you a drink and some bread and cheese. We'll take this lot with us and see how they look in a domestic setting.'

I did not protest or make a pretence of being reluctant to impose on her, for fear that she might find this funny too, but followed her up the straight and narrow staircase to what had no doubt been the bedroom floor when the house was built in the seventeenth century.

It was as well that Robin was not with us, as he and the ceilings were about the same height and he would no doubt have concussed himself on the massive, irregularly shaped beam which supported the sitting room doorway. Also, being honourable by nature, he might not have approved of the methods I used to make myself agreeable.

Since sane people rarely surround themselves with furnishings which they personally find repellent, it is logical to assume that it will generate a bit of goodwill to enthuse about those they have, though it certainly cost an effort this time.

The general impression was not so much ugly or uncomfortable as haphazard. It could have been thrown together by a cynical relative or friend for a blind woman to live in. It would not worry her that the two armchairs were covered in different chintzes, that the sofa cover screamed at both of them and the curtains sagged limply from their hooks.

'How cosy!' I said. 'I love these sloping ceilings.'

I might have known better, of course, and this time Angie did not bother to hide her amusement.

'You know quite well it's shabby and hideous. I shouldn't have been offended if you'd said so.'

65

'Doesn't it bother you?'

'Sometimes. What would you like to drink? I've got everything in the kitchen, but I won't invite you in there. You might say that cracked linoleum and a chipped sink made it look homey. Gin and tonic? Scotch? Sherry?'

'Gin and tonic, please. If it really doesn't bother you, why be on the defensive about it?'

'That's better! Tell you in a minute.'

The drinks came in odd tumblers and mine was very strong.

'Since you ask, one reason why I don't bother with this place or spend any of my hard-earned money on it is that I don't regard it as a permanency. I'd hate to think of being here until I'm carried out feet first.'

'Why should you be?'

'Oh, it's not such a bad job. The money's awful but I run the show in my own way, with the flat thrown in, and I'm not likely to be offered anything better.'

'So why not settle for it?'

'I'm not the settling kind. We're discontented stags, the lot of us, so it must come from my father, I suppose. The reverse side of the coin which drove him on to turn himself from a lower class grammar school boy into a fair imitation of the flower of British aristocracy. Still, at least he was single-minded about it. Decadence set in with the second generation.'

'What form does it take?'

'Soon as we've got what we want we cease to want it.'

'That's a fairly average sort of flaw in every generation.'

'Not when carried to excess. We only cease to want it because we've turned it into something not worth having.'

I considered this observation between sips of gin and tonic, came to the conclusion that there might be some truth in it and that it certainly applied to the third generation. One had only to remember how scruffy and unattractive Steven Westmore managed to appear, despite

66

the wonderful looks he had been born with and, of all the girls I knew, Pam had as much cause as any for contentment with her life and a right old mess she seemed bent on making of it.

'On the other hand,' I said, continuing these unspoken thoughts aloud, 'by one of those strange coincidences, I was lunching with my cousin yesterday and your sister Baba was there. She struck me as being pretty pleased with her lot, more so than most, in fact.'

'Oh, Baba's the worst of all. She wanted a grand title and, having got it, she only needed a couple of years to discover that she couldn't pay the price of living with the man who'd provided it. So she left him and made a laughing stock of herself by hanging on like grim death to the title, when everyone knows she's just plain Mrs Ainslie, subsequently divorced from that one. Her life's been one long farce.'

'She's got a son from each of them.'

'Oh yes, she always gets everything she sets her heart on. She wanted tall, good-looking boys and along they came, but she spoilt them rotten when they were small and now they've grown up she can't accept that they don't need her any more. She's forever chasing after them and trying to run their lives. The result is that one has fled the country and only comes sneaking back when she's away from home and won't find out and the other has become a drop-out and only mixes with the sort of people she despises and fears.'

Although the drawl was now less in evidence, all this had taken several minutes to relate and my glass was almost empty.

'Have another?' she suggested.

'No, thanks, that'll do fine. It was rather powerful and I have to remember not to fall asleep on my way back to London.'

'Oh, you're going to London, are you? I thought you

were probably staying with your aunt. Well, you'd better have a morsel to eat before you leave. Hang on a minute and I'll see what there is in the refrigerator. Take another look at the canvases while you're waiting.'

'I still can't decide,' I admitted, when she returned with a slice of square, limp-looking ham, a tomato cut in half and a wedge of brown bread and butter, 'so I'll take the lot, if that's all right. Aren't you eating anything?'

'No, I've got into the habit of only eating when I'm hungry, which is not very often.'

On the evidence of her emaciated appearance, not to mention the brick-like consistency of the bread, I could believe her.

'I was surprised to hear you say all that about your sister Baba,' I remarked, 'I've rarely met anyone who radiated more self-confidence.'

'Yes, she is inclined to over-estimate herself, always has been. She was the one who could jump higher than anyone else, or swim further, or come out top of her class in the end-of-term exams. When it came to the point it was always too hot to jump or too cold to go in the water and she invariably spent most of exam week in bed, with suspected measles. Underneath all the bravura she has about as much confidence as a three-legged rabbit.'

'Do you see much of her?'

'No more than I can help. I don't suppose she's changed much.'

'I was wondering whether all this talk she goes in for now about publishing her memoirs was also just a show-off?'

'Bound to be. She doesn't have the application or self-discipline to stick at anything for more than a few weeks.'

'That's more or less what one or two other people have told me, but are you certain that it's true in this case?'

'Absolutely. She and I don't communicate much these

days, but I get lengthy reports from my other sister, Dodie. I don't speak to Baba and Baba doesn't speak to me, but Dodie speaks volumes to both of us. It saves a lot of trouble.'

'And it was Dodie who told you that the famous autobiography is just hot air?'

'And she ought to know. She did a lot of typing for Baba, you see, when the idea first raised its head. Reams and reams of it, apparently, mostly about her childhood. But then a few months ago, when the story had got up to the point where Baba went off in tears to her first boarding school, it began to fizzle out and the flow has now dried up. She's obviously reached the stage where it's more fun to talk about herself as an author than go through all the boring slog of actually being one.'

'And do you suppose the letters she now claims to have found are bogus too?'

'Letters?' Angie repeated, the drawl returning in top gear and making the word sound as though it had three syllables. 'What letters?'

'Some your father wrote to a girl he had fallen for in middle age. Didn't Dodie tell you about them?'

'No. . .as a matter of fact, she hasn't rung up during the last couple of weeks. I think she must be away. Who was this girl and how did Baba get hold of the letters?'

'They were found in the attic of a house that had changed hands recently. Before that it had been lived in by a woman who died about six months ago, so presumably they were written to her.'

'Do you know who she was?'

'No. All your sister would tell us was that her name was Elizabeth.'

'Though I suppose it wouldn't be difficult to find out. Did Baba tell you what sort of letters they were?'

'The story of your father's life; or, to be precise, one very unusual part of it. I suppose you can guess what and who it concerned?'

'Oh, she rattled on about all that too, did she?'

'There was nothing indiscreet about it because I already knew most of the story. A good many people do, in a vague, half-forgotten sort of way. Your sister has a different version from the accepted one, though.'

'I know, but hers is a fallacy.'

'That is most people's opinion, but it seems these letters prove her to have been right all along. That's why she's so thrilled and why I'm afraid you under-estimate her in maintaining that the book will never come out. You might as well say that someone who's just been given a brand new car, which she's been dreaming about for years, is never going to take the trouble to learn how to drive it.'

'Being Baba, she would hire a chauffeur to do that for her.'

'My God, I believe you're right. I bet that's just what she has done.'

'Hired a chauffeur?'

'For the book. A ghost, in other words. That's why she doesn't need your sister, Dodie, to do her typing any more. All she'd need to do is record her colourful memories on tape and he'd knock them into narrative form. There are plenty of people who are quite capable of making a presentable job of it.'

'I think I'll get myself another drink,' Angie said, pulling herself up and dawdling over to the door. 'Sure you won't have one?'

'No, thanks,' I said, thinking that two of her drinks on two mouthfuls of bread and ham could spell trouble, 'a glass of water, though, if it's no bother.'

Evidently it was some slight bother because she was away for about five minutes, although she gave no explanation for this and her manner was unchanged when she returned. Nor did she refer to ghost writers, or any other subject, but sat in silence, slowly drinking her gin.

She was one of the few people I had come across who could remain perfectly composed, saying nothing at all when they had nothing to say.

'I must go in a minute,' I said, swallowing the tepid tap water. 'You doubtless have a mass of things lined up for the afternoon, but first of all there's some settling up to do.'

'And we have to find the right wools for three canvases, do we not? Come downstairs and we'll work it out.

'You haven't changed your mind about taking all three?' she asked, as we sorted through rack upon rack of strands of wool for a pink which was something between salmon and rose.

'You think I'm biting off more than I can chew?'

'No, I'm sure you would never do that, but this lot is going to provide you with six months' work. You're not leaving yourself much excuse to come back and ask some more questions.'

'Oh, you've seen through me, have you?' I asked, drifting on to another rack and trying to play it casual.

'Not your fault. I have a suspicious nature. It passed through my mind that you appeared to be unusually interested and well-informed about the antics of my family, but it wasn't until I went into the kitchen that I realised it might have sprung from more than a polite interest.'

'What happened in the kitchen?'

'There's a calendar hanging up beside the sink. I can't think why, because I hardly ever look at it, but I was staring at it while I was filling your glass and I noticed that today was the first Thursday in the month.'

'"Eureka!" you said, as the glass overflowed and the water went swirling down the drain?'

'That's what I said, adding to myself: "Why come all this way for something so trivial on the one day of the month when there's no chance of combining it with a square meal at Aunt Em's?"'

'Perhaps I owe you an apology?'

'Well, I'm curious, I admit. Are you spying for Baba, or what?'

'Not for, on.'

'Oh well, that's something in your favour, I suppose, but you've still wasted your time. You obviously know a lot more about her current activities than I do.'

'I was prepared for that. After all, it's only two days since I talked to her and she's not exactly what you'd call reticent.'

'So what did you come to me for?'

'Well, to be fair, I really did need some more needle-work. I start rehearsing for a film at the end of this month and it's the very thing to pass the long hours of hanging about. Also I was rather hoping to pick up some news of your sister Dodie. That didn't work out either, so I'm taking three canvases as my consolation prize.'

'What did you want to know about Dodie for and why does any of it concern you?'

'It's quite a long story. Do you really want to hear?'

'We'll have some coffee while you tell me. I have all the equipment down here and it's one thing I have learnt how to make properly. Just as well, since I practically live on it.'

'I'll be as brief as I can,' I said when she returned with the steaming mugs, and when I had finished she had only one question:

'More coffee?'

'Yes, please. You were right, it's very good.'

When she came back for the second time I said, 'We've talked about Baba and Dodie, but how about the other three, your half-brother and sisters? Do you still see them?'

'Only Laura. Rita married an Irishman when she was very young and lives somewhere near Waterford, surrounded by about eight children and sixteen grandchildren and approximately the same number of dogs and horses. Baba did make a few overtures and invite herself to stay soon after Rita's father-in-law died and her husband inherited the property and the title, but as far as I know it never came to anything. I still see quite a lot of Laura, though. We sometimes meet for lunch when I have to go to London and she's brought her daughter down here once or twice. Pretty girl, very much like Baba at that age.'

'How about Tom?'

'Oh, Tom! Well, he has come back into our lives to some extent now. Laura's and mine, that is, but we lost touch with him completely when he married and became a bearded wonder, reciting the Psalms all day long.'

'Has he given that up now?'

'Oh no, but his circumstances have changed a bit.'

She seemed unwilling to elaborate on this statement and it was really not my business to probe further into it, so I reverted to the one on which she had been more forthcoming:

'Did you and Laura always get on well?'

'Yes, always. We were more like twins. There's only eight months between us, you see, and it's never really changed much. We didn't go to the same school, but afterwards we spent a year together at RADA. Neither of us stayed the course, as it happens, although I think Laura could have made a go of it. She had far more talent than I had and she was a marvellous mimic, but she lost interest when I got kicked out.'

'And do you look alike too?'

'Not a bit. No one could possibly have mistaken us for identical twins. I take after my mother.'

'And Laura?'

'Her father, like Baba and Rita.'

'What about character?'

'Oh, there we are alike. She's just as vulnerable and

insecure as I am. I don't know who we get that from. Perhaps we're throwbacks.'

'Somehow I wouldn't have described you as vulnerable and insecure, Angie.'

'I've grown an extra skin. It doesn't go very deep, though. That's why, much as I despise Baba for what she plans to do to poor defenceless Laura, I am afraid you must leave me out of your plans. I wish you luck, but I shan't raise a finger to help.'

'Why not?'

'Because, if Baba were to find out that I was trying to spike her guns, it would be just the encouragement she needs to go ahead and, besides, I've got too much to lose by it. My best hope is to lie low and pray to God she loses interest or drops dead before the book is written.'

'Does she really have so much power over you?'

'I think she may have. You might ask your husband. It's the kind of thing he'd be bound to know.'

'What am I to ask him?'

'How many years after someone died can a living person be charged with his murder?'

EIGHT

'Which I suppose was as good as admitting that Baba got it right and Angie did polish off her husband?' I added when I had repeated the question to Robin.

'Although, if she's so scared of its coming out, which is understandable, wasn't it rather ingenuous of her to pass it on to you? Has your friendship already reached the stage where she feels able to trust you with a secret like that?'

'As a matter of fact, we did seem to hit it off fairly well, after the first misunderstanding was cleared up. I liked her and I think it was mutual, but of course the answer to your question is no. The point is, you see, that she had absolutely no means of knowing that I could guess what was in her mind. Now that her mother is dead, she must believe that the only one left who knows about the circumstances of her husband's death is good old Baba. It wouldn't occur to her that Frances would have confided in Aunt Em. They weren't even special friends.'

'So what's your next move?'

'God knows. I'm Yours sincerely, Stuck, to tell you the truth, Robin. Everything now seems to hinge on Dodie. She is the only key I can think of who might open a few more doors – but the key has vanished. I rang up Ellen just before you came in and she tells me there is still no answer from the flat. It was good of her to try, though, because she's racing around in circles, getting ready for the Paris trip. So that means stalemate, at least until Tuesday, when she gets back. The outlook is rather gloomy.'

'Oh, cheer up! You did your best and no one could have worked harder in a more selfless cause.'

'Thank you, but it's not much consolation and what really depresses me is the prospect of having to spend the next three or four days learning my lines, turning out my wardrobe and plodding away at three bits of canvas.'

The boredom of the second and third of these occupations was somewhat alleviated by the radio and this applied particularly to the third. After only two days I had graduated from pop music to quite heavy stuff, like news bulletins and test match commentaries, while plunging my needle in and out of a cluster of strawberries, although I was still a million miles away from the Aunt Em heights of watching television as I did so.

It was during a news report one afternoon that I learnt that a woman had been burnt to death in her cottage in a village called Mallings in Sussex. The fire had started during the night, when she had presumably been in bed and asleep, but the police were not revealing her identity until next of kin had been informed.

It occurred to me that there was something uncanny about this last announcement, for it suggested that Mallings must be quite unlike any village I had personally come across in Sussex, or indeed anywhere else in southern England. How, I asked myself, was it conceivable that anyone living within a three mile radius of the cottage would not be in a position to provide the name, life history and a detailed description of its occupant to any newspaper reporter who cared to ask for them?

The only solution appeared to be that some ban had been imposed either on asking the questions or on printing the answers and, since this was as promising a diversion as had come my way for forty-eight hours, I resolved to keep up to date with the news as it came through during the rest of the afternoon.

The promise could not be kept, however, because during the subsequent edition the number one England fast bowler was being knocked all round the wicket by the number ten batsman, which was too tragic and annoying to be switched off, and I missed the following one too because at ten to six Ellen rang up.

'Anything nice been happening to you?' she asked, having described the wonders and glories of Paris and related several anecdotes to show how wonderful and glorious Jeremy was. 'How's the campaign to muzzle Baba getting on?'

'At a standstill. I thought I was on to something, but it fizzled out. I suppose you haven't had time to try Dodie again?'

'I have, you know. I guessed it would be the first thing you'd ask.'

'No luck, I suppose?'

''Fraid not. I've tried her number twice since I got back, but still no reply.'

'How frustrating! I think I may be forced to abandon that idea, at any rate for the time being, and concentrate on something else.'

'Such as?'

'That's the question, isn't it? Perhaps I could somehow wangle a meeting with Laura and attack the problem from that direction.'

'What's the point of that? You already know how she feels about it, if Derek got it right.'

'I don't know, Ellen, but maybe it could lead to something which just might prove, once and for all, that Baba's story is a myth. On the other hand, perhaps it might just as easily lead to something which showed it was true, in which case we could forget the whole business and let them get on with it. It would be rather an anticlimax, but at least I shouldn't feel that I had totally failed in what I set out to do.'

'Well, don't forget to let me know how you get on. I'll be here till Friday evening and then Jeremy and I are going down to Roakes for the weekend. Why don't you and

Robin come too?'

'That might be fun. I'll ask him how he's fixed and let you know tomorrow.'

By the time we had finished talking six o'clock had come and gone, so I whiled away the next few minutes with a magnifying glass hovering over a section of Robin's very special road map opened out on the floor in front of me.

The object of this labour was to try to discover whether Mallings was anywhere near that particular corner of Sussex where I had a number of friends and relatives with ears close to the ground, but when I tracked it down at last and brought the tape measure out, it turned out to be at least thirty miles nearer to London, not far from a town called Chillingford.

The business of refolding the map in such a way that Robin, for all his trained eye, would never suspect that an alien finger had been laid upon it was made more tedious still by the recurring sensation that there was a faint, familiar ring about the name Chillingford. I eventually dismissed it and renewed my attack on the strawberries by persuading myself that I had once stopped there on my way to somewhere else, though why and with whom was no longer worth trying to remember.

'What news of Derek and Pam?' I asked Robin during dinner.

'Nothing much. One or two minor scares, but the unborn remains alive and kicking, I gather.'

'I thought they might have felt it necessary to invite us back to something or other, after the lovely day we gave them in the country, but perhaps Pam feels her condition is interesting enough to override such petty obligations?'

'I've no doubt she does, but another trouble may be that she feels she would have to lay on something rather magnificent for our benefit. According to Derek, she is

78

very much in awe of you.'

'Oh, nonsense! He made it up to curry favour. At least, if true, she has a funny way of showing it. Practically the only words she addressed to me on Sunday were to ask if we could swop places in the car because the sun was in her eyes. Perhaps the real truth is that you're the one they're in awe of and she doesn't feel it would be *comme il faut* to dish up bangers and mash to Derek's superior officer.'

'Well, why don't we show them how unawful we are by inviting them here one evening for a quiet little drink on their own?'

'I will, if you like, but I'd been hoping to meet Laura Tilling, Pam's mother, and it might sound rather odd to suggest their bringing her too.'

'Curiously enough, it wouldn't, so long as you time it right.'

'What's time got to do with it?'

'Everything, because Laura will shortly be moving in with them. She's sub-let her flat for six months, so as to be permanently on hand. I can't say I altogether approve of the arrangement, but that's their business. The idea is that Pam won't have to be left on her own when Derek has to spend a night away from home, which, as you know, is liable to happen at any time, with practically no warning.'

'When does she move in?'

'Any time now. It was to have been today, but she was spending her last weekend of freedom with some friends in the country and her host has developed a shocking cold, so she's stuck there for a few more days. You can imagine how popular she'd be if she were to go spreading her germs around anywhere near Pam!'

'In that case, Robin, I think it might be worth taking the plunge by getting an extra pound of sausages and inviting a few other people as well. If Laura should turn out to be as boring and neurotic as her daughter, we'll need to spread them a bit thin.'

79

'Yes, if you like.'

'So how about next Sunday? I know it's not your favourite evening for parties, with the start of a new week looming over you, but you'll be able to give Derek the signal when you've had enough and, if he knows what's good for him, that should break things up.'

'You seem to have got it all worked out.'

'Only the broad outline. I shall fill in the details when you've spoken to Derek and get everything organised before we go to Roakes on Saturday.'

'Are we going to Roakes on Saturday?'

'Not if you'd rather not, but Ellen and Jeremy will be there, so Toby will need all the support we can give him. He can't stand Jeremy, as you know, and can never understand what Ellen sees in him.'

'Then I certainly think you should go on your own, even if I can't get away. It will provide a harmless outlet for your passion for interfering in other people's lives. God knows what mayhem we could be in for if you're forced to languish at home for another two or three days.'

These matters having banished all thoughts of news bulletins for that evening, it was not until nine o'clock the following morning, when I opened the newspaper which Robin had deposited on the bed before going out, that I was able to catch up with the story of the woman who had been burnt to death in a Sussex village. It contained two surprises, neither, for some reason which eluded me, quite as surprising as it should have been.

The report was on an inside page and consisted of no more than half a dozen lines. In the first the victim was named as Mrs Dorothy Watson and the bottom one stated that the possibility of arson had not been ruled out.

NINE

Later on I telephoned Ellen to ask for Dodie's surname, but for once she could not oblige.

'Something quite ordinary, as far as I can remember. It seemed to suit her, if you know what I mean. She is one of those women who are destined to be known throughout their lives as someone else's daughter or wife.'

After a pause, she added doubtfully, 'Want me to ask Baba?'

'No, I don't think that would do at all. If, by some remote chance, my guess is right, questions of that kind could land you in deep water. On the other hand, if it's wrong it wouldn't serve any purpose to know Dodie's surname.'

'And it's such a very long shot, isn't it? There must be thousands of women of that generation called Dorothy.'

'Very true, Ellen, but there was something else in the story which struck a chord long before I heard the name.'

'Oh, really? What was that?'

'Chillingford. I looked up Mallings on the map, you see, to find out exactly where it was and it turned out to be a few miles from a town called Chillingford. What does that remind you of?'

'Chingford or Chelmsford, I suppose.'

'And aren't they precisely what might have occurred to Baba, if she was purposely being vague, but, guarding against all possibilities, wanted it to sound like the sort of natural mistake anyone might make?'

'Perhaps. What do we do now, then? Just wait and see, presumably?'

'Nothing else for it,' I agreed, 'although I don't propose to wait a minute longer than I have to.'

My next call was to Robin, to find out what response he had had from Derek about Sunday evening. He told me that the invitation had been provisionally accepted on behalf of all three.

'That's good,' I said. 'It means that I can go ahead with the rest of my plans. I hope to be in a position to present you with the full cast list this evening. In the meantime, could you do something else for me?'

'Usual proviso. Depends what it is.'

'Could you find out something about the background of a woman who died in a fire in Sussex, the night before last? West Sussex it would be. Name of Dorothy Watson.'

'I don't know. Can you give me a few more details?'

I did so and his reply was much the same as Ellen's: 'Sorry, nothing doing.'

'Oh, why not?'

'Use your loaf! Officially, I can't go barging in at this stage, it would be most unethical. And, if I tried to do it unofficially, I should get no more out of them than you would, which would be nothing.'

'Oh well, can't be helped. I shall just have to press on with my social engagements and have another bash at the strawberries.'

Clarrie was next on my list and luckily she had no matinee, so I waited until five o'clock, when I estimated that she would be at home, getting ready to leave for the theatre.

'Can you ... er ... both come to dinner on Sunday evening?' I asked, realising too late that I had forgotten her husband's name.

'Love to, darling, but Denis is in Australia. Or somewhere like that.'

'I don't think there is anywhere quite like that; but come on your own, in that case.'

'Wouldn't it break your heart to have an extra female?'

'Not at all, it's not that sort of party. But bring someone else, if you like. How about that young man we met in your room the other evening?'

'Steven? Well, no, I doubt if I'll be doing that.'

'Why not? Have you gone off him?'

'Certainly not, he's one of my dearest friends. It's just that he's heavily involved in some family drama at the moment. His revolting mother is carrying on like a lunatic and can't bear the darling boy to leave her side for a single second.'

'What's it all about, do you know?'

'Some aunt has died, I gather. Her house caught on fire and she was trapped inside. Apparently Baba doesn't regard that as a suitable way for a well-bred person to be gathered and she's flinging her weight about, trying to get it hushed up.'

'Bless you, Clarrie!'

'Whatever for, in God's name?'

'Tell you on Sunday, maybe. I expect you'll be able to find another escort without too much trouble?'

'I don't know about that. What sort of people will you be having?'

'All sorts. Pros, members of the Metropolitan Police Force, young middle-aged and in-between, like you and me.'

'Speak for yourself, I feel a hundred. Okay, I'll see what I can do and ring you back some time.'

By ten o'clock the next morning I had almost begun to feel sorry for Baba. Full details of Mrs Dorothy Watson's antecedents and more respectable living relatives had now been released to the press and, if she had been hoping that her own connection with the deceased would be played down, if not suppressed altogether, they must have made unpleasant reading.

In fact, it was she, rather than the victim, who emerged as the principal character in this drama, great stress being laid on the fact that she was known to the world as Barbara, Marchioness of Doverfield, considerably less on her legal status as Mrs Ainslie.

She had tried hard to evade the reporters, but, inevitably, that battle had been lost before it had started and by four o'clock she had run straight into the clutches of about twenty of them. They had greeted her as she alighted from a taxi outside the house of a friend with whom she had sought refuge and who had presumably telephoned every newspaper and television editor in London half an hour before she turned up. My compassion was mitigated, however, by the reflection that she had most likely set fire to the cottage herself, with the express purpose of ensuring that the wretched Dodie would perish in the flames.

Aside from this aspect of the matter, the most piquant element of the affair was contained in that part of the interview in which Baba replied to a near-impertinent question about her relationship with her dead sister. She said that they had not met for several weeks, as she had been so busy working on her book, but that they were a very close family and regularly communicated by telephone. She knew about the cottage in Sussex, which was a recent acquisition, but had been surprised to learn that her sister had gone there only a few days ago, having gained the impression that she was proposing to spend a few weeks with an old friend in Denmark.

The real *coup de grâce*, or series of varying sizes of coups, was delivered by Robin when he arrived home from work just after seven.

'I can now speak freely,' he announced, 'or relatively freely, at any rate. Although I suppose it has come too late

84

to be of much use to you. I imagine you have heard all you wanted to know from other voices?'

'Not quite all. What has conferred this freedom on you?'

'A slight case of mistaken identity. Outside help is now urgently required to deal with it. So I no longer have to keep my distance.'

'Does that mean you've been put in charge?'

'Not me, no, for which I'm thankful because I obviously wouldn't have been able to have Derek on my team and we've got used to each other's funny ways now.'

'Whose identity got mistaken?'

'The woman who was burnt to death in the cottage. She turns out not to have been Mrs Dorothy Watson after all. Or, at any rate, not the one we have all been reading about in the newspapers.'

'I don't believe it! Are you sure? How could anyone have made such a foolish mistake?'

'Well, there was some excuse, as it happens, bearing in mind that there wasn't much left to identify by the time she was found. They ought to have waited for the forensic team to confirm it, but they didn't and, as I say, there was some excuse for jumping to the wrong conclusion.'

'So who was it?'

'That is the big question, to which the answer has still to be found.'

'But how incredible! And, if they can't tell from the remains who it was, how can they be so sure who it wasn't?'

'Oh, Dodie provided the answer to that one.'

'No! You don't mean to tell me that Baba's story was true?'

'I thought that would rock you. It took a bit of unravelling, but they got there in the end.'

'Got where?'

'In the course of some routine enquiries, as the saying goes, Baba was questioned about her sister's movements

85

during the past few days and she replied, quite unneces-
sarily, I might say, that she could not swear to it on oath,
but she believed she was staying with an old friend in
Denmark, which she invariably did at this time of year.
She was unable to supply the address of this friend, or even
her full name, only that she was called Ingrid or Inge.
However, since by this time other evidence had come to
light, all pointing to its being Dodie who had died, they
concluded that Baba had got it wrong. Not from a wish to
mislead them, or because she was deliberately concealing
anything, you understand, but simply, they thought, from
lack of interest in anything which did not directly concern
herself.'

'And who shall blame them?'

'Quite so, but unfortunately it was they who'd got it
wrong. At five o'clock this evening the real Mrs Watson
stood up to telephone the news that she was alive,
comparatively well and living in Copenhagen, where
some of the English papers are on sale by midday.'

'Why only comparatively?'

'She had fallen downstairs and broken her ankle, but
hoped to be in a fit state to travel by the end of next week.'

'Well, I'm damned! And when you said other evidence
had come to light, what was that all about? What sort of
evidence?'

'Not the positive kind. It would be truer to say that it
did nothing to suggest that she was not the woman in
question.'

'Which leaves me none the wiser.'

'The cottage, Fairview it's called, is not particularly
isolated, you see, although it clearly was when it was built
a couple of hundred years ago. Since then Mallings has
grown to about four times its original size and the view
nowadays is mainly of new developments and housing
estates. Unfortunately, people who live in such surroundings tend to be birds of passage. They have no roots, take

no part in local activities and have little interest in the neighbours, outside their own particular group. Nevertheless, two or three of them were able to come up with some scraps of information about the tenant of Fairview.'

'Like what?'

'Like the fact that Mrs Watson, although most of them didn't know or had forgotten her name, had moved in a few months ago and that on one or two occasions there had been a man with her, so perhaps there lies the answer to her mysterious comings and goings.'

'How did they describe her?'

'Ordinary, dull, middle-aged and dowdy about covers it.'

'And the man?'

'Same type. Ordinary, medium height, clean-shaven. The only deviation from this refrain came from a woman who said she had assumed him to be Mrs Watson's son, although she couldn't define her reason for thinking so.'

'How about postmen and all that?'

'No good. She didn't receive any letters at all, beyond an occasional circular addressed to the occupant, and she had one of those mailboxes in the porch. So it made no difference whether she was there or not when they were delivered. The best hope seemed to be the taxi, but that was a wash-out too.'

'What taxi?'

'The one that brought her to the cottage each time and collected her again. Black, not new, with a light on the roof. They all assumed, reasonably enough, that it was a station cab.'

'But they were wrong?'

'Not necessarily, but from which station? is the question. The nearest one on the main line, with fast trains to Victoria, is at Chillingford, which is only four miles away. One taxi firm has the concession, so it should have been a matter of hours to get a full, first-hand description of the

87

so-called Mrs Watson and, with a bit of luck, she might have paid by cheque. As it turned out, though, not one of the drivers remembered ever having driven to that address in Mallings.'

'Perhaps she bribed them to keep it dark?'

'Not very likely. There are more than a dozen of them and she couldn't have relied on getting the same one each time. Besides, they have to hand in detailed records of every job at the end of the shift, so any hanky-panky could soon be detected.'

'So what are the alternatives?'

'They're endless. Perhaps she didn't come from London, but made a cross-country journey which landed her up at some station further afield. Redhill, for instance. That has connections with Brighton and several other coastal towns. On the other hand, maybe she was one of those people who have a phobia about trains. In which case, she could have hired the cab and driven the whole way from wherever she lived. Or, if it was from any great distance away, the question would be, whatever she was up to, why not have chosen a more accessible place than Mallings for it? Why travel for miles two or three times a month, just to hide herself away for a few days?'

'Well, I suppose that's the big question, wherever she came from. And what exactly was she up to is an even bigger one, in my opinion.'

'You are not alone.'

'Have they established yet whether it was arson or not?'

'Still working on it, but that's a tough one too. The fire appears to have started upstairs, which is not the usual way to go about things, particularly when the house is occupied. Assuming, of course, that it wasn't an elaborate form of suicide.'

'Didn't anyone from the housing estate notice anything?'

'Not soon enough, apparently. It was dead of night,

about four in the morning to be precise, when the call came through to the Chillingford Fire Brigade and the cottage had evidently been burning merrily for some hours. When they arrived on the scene the staircase had gone and, since there were no signs of life from upstairs, they concluded the house had been empty when it started. Quite natural, in the circumstances. There was no car in the garage, but the telephone was connected, so if anyone had been at home they'd been unusually slow about calling for help. Anyway, that's about all I can tell you at present, so let's move on to that other burning topic. Who's coming to the party on Sunday evening?'

I rattled off half a dozen names of those who had accepted, plus the same number, including Clarrie, who were still hovering, and when we had written and rewritten the menu about four times, I said, 'Just one more question before I put the potatoes on and grill our steak for tonight.'

'Oh, haven't we settled everything?'

'This is going back to the other burning question. I meant to ask you before, but it got lost. Couldn't the agents who rented the house to Mrs Watson come up with some information about her?'

'Not a lot and it did more to confuse than clarify the issue.'

'But at least they saw her and knew what she looked like?'

'Only once. Middle-aged, quiet, ladylike and reserved is the picture which once again emerges and it could apply to millions of women. This one walked in one morning and told them she wanted a small place to rent furnished for a few months, while she looked around for something in the neighbourhood to buy for her retirement, which was coming up in a year's time. They had only two possibilities on their books and she chose this one and paid a deposit of three months' rent in advance.'

'By cheque?'

'In cash.'

'Isn't that unusual?'

'Not particularly, nowadays.'

'No references?'

'Yes, several. Bank manager, current landlord. All quite impeccable.'

'But surely that would have...I'm getting confused, Robin. You can't mean....?'

'Yes, I can. The deal was done in cash, but the references were taken up and replied to in writing.'

'And the lease was signed in the name of...?'

'Dorothy Watson, of course.'

'Address?'

'Can't you guess? That very flat in Bayswater where the real Dorothy Watson lives. The one who is now in Denmark and who swears she has never set foot in Mallings in her life. So now you can see how the mistake occurred when the charred remains of a female were found inside the burnt-out cottage?'

'Unless, of course, it wasn't a mistake at all and the Dorothy Watson in Denmark is the impostor?'

'I'd say that was even more improbable. Apart from the complication of passport and visa and so on, the Denmark Dorothy is due to present herself to the authorities next week and it is rather more difficult to impersonate a live woman than a dead one.'

'Maybe she won't turn up?'

'Well, that, of course, would present a fresh set of problems. In the meantime, it might be better to concentrate on more pressing and practical matters.'

'Such as?'

'Oh, laying in stocks of food and wine for the party, deciding how many suitcases you'll need to see you through one night at Roakes Common.'

'Yes, you're right. Nothing like a few routine chores for

90

letting the mind roam free, but before we close the conversation for tonight, just one more question, please!'

Robin sighed. 'I knew that pretence of surrender was too good to be true. What now?'

'You mentioned a station that Dorothy Watson might have used if she'd been travelling cross-country. Which one was it?'

'Redhill. It's only fourteen miles away and it's quite an important junction on the southern region. Why do you want to know?'

'I really can't tell you. Some bell seemed to ring when you mentioned it the first time, but it's been muffled now. Perhaps it'll come to me as I pack.'

Clarrie kept up the suspense until Saturday morning. I had all but crossed her off my list when the telephone rang at ten.

'Verily and after all, the lord cometh,' she announced in gloomy tones.

Recognising the mood as the sombre one which often prompts her to revert to the tenor of conversation in her father's parsonage and hoping to shake her out of it, I said brightly, 'Oh, good! You mean Steven, I take it?'

'That's the one. Not that he'll be much of an asset, I should warn you. He's a good-hearted boy and can be very nice on his own, but a bit of an aching bore when two or three are gathered together. He does not toil to make himself amusing and neither does he spin. Still, it was your idea to invite him and it now turns out that his mother has no need of him on Sunday evening. Apparently, it wasn't his aunt who died the other day, it was someone else. You wouldn't think anyone could make that sort of mistake, would you?'

'No, but they're quite an odd family and I suppose it's quite a common name.'

'What is?'

'Dorothy Watson, the woman who was killed in a fire and also the name of Baba's sister.'

'Oh, really? Fancy that! You always know everything, don't you, Tessa?'

'Well, it's no secret. Don't you read the papers?'

'God, no. Only reviews.'

'Well, it's been splashed all over them, mainly because

for a brief moment she was assumed to be the daughter of that well-known playwright whose work you have been so gustily breathing new life into. How's it going, by the way?'

'Beautifully. Packed out for every performance. We could have extended the run again, but they want the theatre for something else, which is pretty devastating and annoying.'

'May be just as well, though. You'd have got frightfully bored with it if you'd gone on much longer.'

'I shall get frightfully bored without it, if you want to know. I am facing a blank page in my life.'

My sixth sense should have been wide awake at this point because Clarrie has a curious chemical reaction to boredom and the result can be similar to dynamite in the hands of a lunatic, but, with more pressing matters in mind, I brushed off her last remark by saying, 'Oh, cheer up! We all do that sometimes and you'll soon find something amusing written on yours. Tell me something, Clarrie; did Steven's mother genuinely believe it was her sister who was dead? Or was she just putting on an act to get her beloved boy's attention?'

'Hard to say. About half and half, probably.'

'You mean she half believed it and half didn't?'

'No, I meant that she did believe it, but most of the agony was put on. She really didn't give much of a damn. That's Steven's view, anyway, and I should think he must be right. It's the only way it makes sense.'

'It doesn't make sense to me, I have to tell you.'

'Well, the fact is, when they told her it wasn't her sister after all, she really went berserk. Tearing her hair out by the handful. You can see that something's annoyed her, so it's most likely that she can't any longer play the poor, bereaved heroine.'

'But listen, Clarrie, you told me just now that you'd be bringing Steven to the party because everything had

93

calmed down.'

'I did nothing of the kind, you make it up as you go along. What I said was that he'd been let off her hook for the nonce. She has bigger fish to fry. The other one is coming over and he'll be here this evening.'

'The son in California?'

'That's right. Perry, he's called. Short for Peregrine, in case you hadn't guessed. When she was wailing the dirge of grief-stricken sister, she sent for him and by the time the correction came in he was halfway to New York and too late to alter course. He'll probably be furious when he discovers that his journey wasn't necessary, which may be why she feels it would be more diplomatic not to let him find Steven installed there, holding her hand and waving the smelling salts.'

'As well she might, but what I find harder to understand is why someone would be mildly exasperated to learn that her sister had been burnt to death and utterly wretched to discover that she had not.'

'Don't ask me, darling, I'm the last one to understand how her mind works. She pretended to be furious about all the horrid, vulgar publicity, but I suppose she was secretly revelling in it. She even managed to palm one of the reporters off with a photograph of herself, looking like a circus pony when she was presented at court.'

'All the same, I should think there must be more to it than that, wouldn't you?' I asked Ellen, as we strolled over the Common later that day.

'Meaning that she arranged for the house to be burnt down when she believed Dodie would be in it and then found it wasn't Dodie after all, but someone else? Like sticking pins in a wax figure and finding you'd made the wrong image?'

'Funnily enough, you said something like that once before.'

94

'Did I? I don't remember.'

'You were only twelve at the time.'

'And is that what happened?'

'In a sense, yes, but somehow I can't see Baba making a mistake like that. She may be a hot air balloon, but I'd say her feet were firmly on the ground. She seems to know exactly what she wants and how to get it and I'm sure if she ever contrived something of that sort she'd have every detail worked out in advance.'

'Well, even the best-laid plans . . .'

'Oh, I know and, anyway, none of it gets us any nearer to knowing who was killed. That's the real mystery.'

'I suppose it's only a question of time, though, isn't it? Sooner or later, the police are bound to come up with the answer.'

'I'm not so sure. I don't see how they can get very far unless someone reports a missing person who corresponds to what little is known about this one. Then I suppose it might be proved that they were one and the same.'

'Isn't it strange that no one has done that already?'

'Not necessarily, if it was not in their interest to do so. She may have been dead before the fire started. They can't even establish that much.'

'But listen, Tessa, if she was somebody who knew Dodie well enough to be able to use her name and address and all the other details when she signed the lease, it must mean that she also knew, or had taken the trouble to find out a hell of a lot about the whole Seymour clan. Surely that makes it easier to track her down?'

'My God, Ellen, you're right, of course! How clear-sighted of you! I simply hadn't thought of it from that point of view. You see what it means?'

'I thought it meant what I said.'

'Yes, indeed, but, looking a bit beyond that, can't you see how it could turn every one of our theories about Baba on its head? Furthermore, it might explain why she was

95

only moderately put out to learn that her sister had been killed and really started climbing up the wall when she discovered the sister was alive and well in Copenhagen?'

'Well, naturally I'm delighted that my clear-sightedness has achieved all that, but I can't really understand how you work it out.'

'It's the letters, don't you see? It must mean that you and I were wrong to suspect Baba of having invented them and that, after all, they did exist and were perfectly genuine. Well, perhaps that's going too far, but at any rate she believed in their existence and was banking everything on their turning out to be genuine. That's why her hair has now turned white overnight and she's pulling it out in handfuls. It's not the human victim she's worried about, whoever it may be. She's wild with disappointment because she thinks her precious letters have gone up in flames. In other words, it has now sunk in that this may very well be the cottage where Elizabeth corresponded with Sheridan. If you remember, she told us that the only address she had was a poste restante at Chelmsford or Chingford, so the name Mallings would have meant nothing to her until those maps of the area round Chillingford started appearing on the television screens.'

'I expect you're right as usual, Tessa, and, if you are, it might also explain why she sent out the mayday call to Peregrine.'

'Why? What's the connection there?'

'Well, it's put her in a bit of a fix, hasn't it? All those poor overworked policemen searching high and low for a clue to this mystery woman's identity and Baba may be the one person in the whole country who can provide it. I'm sure she's not at all eager to get involved, specially if there's still a chance the letters have been moved to a safe hiding place. On the other hand, if she lies low and lets things take their course and then the full story comes out later, she'll be in a right mess. Prosecuted for withholding

96

evidence, for all I know. Anyway, a bad blow to her image – and you know how vain she is.'

'And you think that's why she sent for Peregrine?'

'Wouldn't surprise me. Obviously, she'd need to talk it over in confidence with someone who'd give her sound advice and Steven would be no use at all. He's incapable of giving advice to somebody standing too near the edge of a cliff and you couldn't trust him with a baby's rattle.'

'But Peregrine's different, is he? Have you met him?'

'Oh, you bet! When he was about sixteen and I was still sticking pins in wax figures. Nowadays he likes to pretend that he's always been madly in love with me, but it's only a game. He'd have run a mile if I'd responded.'

'Apart from that, what's he like?'

'Very satisfactory, from Baba's point of view. Marvellous looks, very ambitious, tough as boots and given to wearing his old school tie. Her very own dream boy, in fact.'

I was interested by this description, which was one which many people would have applied to Jeremy, and was pondering whether it was purely the attraction of opposites which prompted such men to fall for Ellen or whether the cause went deeper than that, when she recalled me to business by remarking thoughtfully:

'In a way, I suppose it's landed you and me in a bit of a fix too?'

'I get your drift,' I replied, 'but I see no reason to float along with it. Just because Baba took her hair down with us doesn't put us under any obligation to repeat what she told us to anyone else, whatever it might do to further the cause of justice. For one thing, if you recall, she never actually mentioned Mallings or Chillingford, so it's based on guesswork, anyway. Secondly, if she could babble away like that to two females half her age and one of them a complete stranger, it's a safe bet that she'd already babbled away to countless other people.'

'I'm not sure you're right there, Tessa.'

'Why not? Why would she have picked on us and no one else?'

'Mainly, I should think, because we listened. What you may not have taken in yet is that she's been obsessed by this book of hers for years now and it's become a stale joke. People lay odds on how long it will take her to drag it into the conversation and when she does they more or less switch off and fall into a coma until they find a decent excuse to change the subject. So you can imagine the effect when you and I sat there, wide-eyed and gobbling up every word.'

'Quite intoxicating, I suppose.'

'Yes, literally. She was like someone who'd had a couple of drinks too many. I bet she regretted it afterwards too and is now thanking God on her knees that at least she didn't mention Chillingford or Elizabeth's surname.'

'Although that may have been her good luck. I daresay she genuinely had forgotten them. However, I do begin to see what you mean.'

'And you feel you might be duty bound to pass it on to Robin?'

'It poses a delicate moral question. After all, he's in possession of most of the facts already. Not all, but enough to work out the connection for himself.'

'He may have had other things on his mind.'

'No doubt and that's the point, Ellen. If he were on this case himself he'd snap up any stray piece of information that came his way, including gossip, hearsay and rumour, but he's not and he wouldn't even be in line for the honour and glory of solving it. I really think we're entitled to keep our ideas to ourselves for another few days; at least until after the party.'

We were approaching the garden gate by this time and she said, 'I noticed you haven't invited Jeremy and me to your party.'

'You can come if you like. It never occurred to me that you'd want to.'

'But you invited Dad.'

'Who says so?'

'He does. He says there aren't many social events that would induce him to spend Sunday evening in London, but he's quite looking forward to this one.'

I did not allow it to turn my head, for anyone who knew Toby might have guessed that he had settled for the slightly lesser of two evils. Accepting non-existent invitations would be one way to forestall any plans Jeremy might have for staying on till Monday.

He had reckoned without Ellen, however, and it came as quite a relief to discover that, after all, she was not wholly untainted by the devious streak either.

'I don't think we will come, thanks all the same,' she said, as we walked up the path. 'As a matter of fact, since Dad will be away tomorrow evening, we thought we might stay till Tuesday and recuperate from all the stamping round galleries and shops in Paris. Jeremy's devoted to him, as you know, but in some ways he finds it more comfortable when he's not here and we both feel he's getting badly stuck in his rut. So, you see, Tess, if you were able to find some excuse to keep him in London for an extra day, you'd be doing us all a favour.'

ELEVEN

Derek, with his wife and mother-in-law, were the first to arrive, which Robin's own high standard of punctuality may have had something to do with. Personally, I am more open-minded on the subject. It can certainly be a virtue in a dentist, whose patients are trapped in his chilly waiting room, but dinner guests who have been invited for eight o'clock and arrive five minutes before the hour leave something to be desired.

However, I consoled myself for the worry of all those last-minute jobs which ought to have been done and were still undone by the thought that it would at least provide me with the chance for a little study and quizzing of Laura before other demands came crowding in.

Early signs were not propitious, for she gave the impression of a woman whose whole life had been spent in a back seat and who had ended by making herself very comfortable in it. Certainly, she was in no danger of being ousted by her daughter. Pam had entered the room ahead of the other two, had been the first to sit down and had piped up her request for a straight orange juice, whatever that might be, before Robin had completed the question. She was wearing a dark blue yoked tent for this occasion, with a white lace collar, a combination which made her look heavily pregnant and also demure and virginal, which was very touching and effective.

Another impediment to direct conversation with Laura was that, inevitably, after two or three minutes, Derek drifted over to join Robin at the bar, where they instantly fell into a deep and muffled discussion on subjects of no interest to anyone but themselves. So, stuck with a three-way conversation, I compromised by asking questions of a general nature, while watching Laura, who was watching Pam, who was answering them.

After half a dozen rounds of this I began to have the uncomfortable sensation of being out-manoeuvred at my own game and that, although Laura kept her eyes on Pam, in fact most of her attention was focussed on me. So when we had heard all about the pre-natal exercise class, which took place every Wednesday and was always so exhausting, I changed course and asked Laura, 'Do you find yourself automatically observing people you meet and storing their characteristics away for future reference?'

'No, never. Not consciously, that is. Why do you ask?'

'I thought it might be a trick which authors would acquire, perhaps almost without realising it. Then one day, when it's needed, up pops one of those recollections and comes in handy.'

'What a charming idea! And perhaps it does apply to fiction writers. Alas, my books are largely about real people and they're based on dull things like research. Also most of them belong to much earlier periods than our own, so contemporary speech and fashions are no use to me. In fact, I try to cut myself off from them, as far as possible.'

I could imagine that she succeeded pretty well, on the whole. Although in appearance Laura was a watered-down and prim-looking version of Baba, if I had closed my eyes it could have been Angie speaking and I marvelled that anyone should describe either of them as insecure and defenceless. Encased, as they both appeared to be, in their self-sufficiency and indifference to the opinion of others, they struck me as rather less vulnerable than most.

Switching to a more neutral subject, I said, 'Robin tells me you've been staying in the country. It must have been lovely in this weather, or did you have to spend long hours helping your hosts with the watering?'

'No, far from it, I'm sorry to say. The so-called garden is scarcely larger than this room and they don't bother to keep it up because they're trying to sell the house. Besides, it's not in what you could call real country.'

'Suburban, you mean?'

'No, not that either. One of those amorphous developments which sprang up along the south coast between the wars.'

'Oh, I know! And they all have lovely names like Peacehaven and things like that?'

'This one is called Beachclyffe, as it happens, which is also a misnomer, since there are no cliffs and it's at least half a mile from the sea.'

'How curious!'

'Not really. As you say, most of them have these inappropriate and rather misleading names.'

'Yes, I'm sure, but the curious part is that the parents of a friend of mine have retired to a place called Beachclyffe. She hasn't got a car and I've promised to drive her down there to lunch with them one day. Carson, they're called. I wonder if your friends know them, by any chance?'

'I shouldn't think so. They don't mix much with the neighbours,' Laura said in a bored voice and then turned her head away to look round the room, as though the subject were now exhausted.

However, I was saved from having to dig around for a new one by the entrance at this moment of several more guests, including Toby. Others followed hot on their heels, so, having commanded him to go and find something to say to Laura as a punishment for his duplicity and ascertained that Robin and Derek had broken up their private conference, I sped to the kitchen to add the final touches to the arrangements for dinner.

Robin joined me there a few minutes later, ostensibly to ask if I needed help.

102

'No, thanks. Mrs Cheeseman is managing splendidly. She's gone to put the salad and stuff out in the dining room and all the hot things are in the oven. Should be ready in about twenty minutes, if that suits.'

'Sooner the better, I should think,' he replied glumly, nibbling the discarded end of a cucumber. 'Clarrie's here.'

'What's that got to do with it? Is she starving or something?'

'You could say that. And, while we're on the subject, I'm not sure it was a terribly good idea of yours to invite that oaf, Steven.'

'I didn't exactly invite him, it sort of fell out that way. And, besides, why should anyone mind? If Laura can be friendly with her half-sister Angie, what's to stop Pam being friendly with her half-cousin Steven?'

'I wasn't worried about those two. I'm afraid the real trouble is that Clarrie's bored with him.'

The minute I re-entered the room I understood exactly what he meant and why he had considered it appropriate to describe Clarrie as starving. I had been half prepared for this because it had not escaped me that she had reached the stage where, having gobbled up Steven, she was about ready to spit him out and find herself another poor fish to fry. What I had not foreseen was that the first one to start leaping to the bait would be Derek.

Perhaps it was inevitable, though. Of all the half dozen or so men in the room, he was the youngest, apart from Steven, and among the most presentable. More to the point, he was virgin territory, the only one she had never set eyes on before and the eye he was setting on her in return must have held all the promise she could have asked for.

It was not that he had ceased to love Pam with the same single-minded devotion, any more than it can be said of a drunken man that he does not intend to reach the door simply because he has become incapable of approaching it in a straight line. Furthermore, as I knew of old, Clarrie kept a special trick up her sleeve for these occasions, somehow contriving to make her victim feel that he was doing her an enormous favour by engaging her in conversation and that, but for him, she would be exposed to the humiliation of standing lonely as a cloud and watching the party go by without her.

Clearly, though, Pam could not be expected to understand any of this and, judging by her tight-lipped expression, I did not consider I would improve matters by trying to explain it to her. Nor, in this situation, would I have been a match for Clarrie. Any attempt on my part to break up her tête-à-tête would instantly have been recognised as a sign that her behaviour was liable to cause friction and heartbreak and would have encouraged her to turn up the heat a degree or two higher.

So when I had darted out to the kitchen to ask Mrs Cheeseman whether she could possibly bring the dinner forward by five or ten minutes, I literally dragged Robin out of a conversation with two other people and hissed at him to go and put a stop to Clarrie's game.

'What do you expect me to do about it?' he asked, none too pleased.

The tactful answer, of course, would have been that he was the last man in the world to need instruction on how to engage the attention of an attractive harpy, but I was in no mood for clever tactics. 'Oh, how the hell would I know? Fling your arms round her and say that I don't understand you, or that you hate the colour of her hair, or anything that comes into your head. Only just break it up, for God's sake, otherwise we'll have a miscarriage on our hands, if not worse.'

'Oh, very well, but don't say I didn't warn you.'

It seemed, however, that Laura had forestalled him, making his task unnecessary and, as he walked reluctantly towards his prey, there came a terrified, high-pitched scream from Pam.

'Oh, God! Oh, Mummy, what is it, what's the matter? Oh, do something, somebody, for God's sake! Can't you see she's going to die?'

Everyone stopped talking and Toby, who had probably been asleep with his eyes open, opened them wider still and hastily backed away, revealing Laura in her corner going through a strange and alarming form of mime. She was sitting bolt upright, with her back as rigid as a telegraph pole but with arms flapping ever more weakly, and she appeared to be holding her breath while counting to a thousand. Her mouth was wide open, but no sound came from it. Only her tear-filled eyes, bulging from her reddening face, implored us to rescue her from whatever catastrophe had come upon her.

Fortunately, this was the kind of contretemps in which Robin felt more at home and one glance had told him what was wrong and what should be done about it. Stationing himself behind her chair, he delivered such a thumping blow between her shoulder blades that she fell forward like a stone and I was half afraid that he had decided that the merciful solution was to put her out of her misery by killing her on the spot.

She was alive, however, and, if not in the pink of health, was at least breathing and with her complexion returning to its normal colour.

'All right now?' he asked, as she slowly raised her head and sank back in her seat.

'Yes . . . thank . . . you,' she replied in spaced-out gasps, 'I do . . . apologise. How fortunate you knew what to do . . . otherwise, I don't think I could . . . have survived this one. It's over now, Pam, nothing to worry about, so do stop crying, darling. It's so bad for you.'

'You've had these attacks before, then?' Robin asked.

'Only once, many years ago. Not so bad as this one,

though. May I have a glass of water, Tessa?'

'Yes, of course, right away,' I replied and, getting up, called out to the multitude that all was now well, they could relax and prepare to eat their dinner in ten or fifteen minutes.

Having handed over the glass of water, I left Robin in charge and retrod the well-beaten path to the kitchen, to ask Mrs Cheeseman if she would kindly hold up the dinner for another quarter of an hour. This did not go down very well, so I added that, if she felt like giving notice, I should have every sympathy, but should be obliged if she could put it off until the morning, when I hoped to be in a better state to receive the news calmly.

When I returned Clarrie was in her element, flapping her eyelids and dispensing drinks and merry quips to a group of male admirers, while the rest of the party huddled about in a leaden hush. Laura was still leaning back with her eyes closed and Pam was still whining and snivelling, while Robin and Derek stood about looking as though they wished they were somewhere else.

'Wouldn't it be better if Derek took Pam home now?' I suggested.

'We think it would,' Robin agreed, 'but she refuses to leave without her mother.'

'Oh, I see! Well, in that case, perhaps they'd both be more comfortable in one of the bedrooms?'

Pam was heard to mumble that she ought not to climb any stairs because she had a funny sort of pain coming on and Laura, still with her eyes closed, murmured, 'Please don't worry about us. Just give me a few more minutes and I shall be all right to go home.'

Silence fell again and this time it was Steven, of all people, who shambled into the breach.

'Take her myself, if you like,' he announced in his truculent way. 'The other two can go ahead and we'll follow when she's ready.'

106

'Oh, that's awfully kind of you, Steven. Are you sure you don't mind. The only thing is, though . . . have you got a car, or what?'

'Not an or what, a car. It's Clarrie's, but she won't mind. I'll bring it back.'

'Yes, I'm sure you will, but, all the same, we'd better ask her. Come with me.'

As I spoke, I heard scuffling noises in the background, and, turning round, saw that Laura had struggled to her feet.

'Very kind of you,' she said, sounding more cross than grateful, 'but I wouldn't dream of putting you to all that trouble and I'm feeling much, much better now. Come along, Pam, there's a good girl. Derek's going to take us home now.'

As a curtain line it lacked something because it then took at least another five minutes to get Pam into a semblance of the perpendicular and out of the room, supported on either side by mother and husband. Robin followed a pace or two behind, looking like the chief mourner at a funeral.

After they had gone the party creaked and lumbered on, but it never regained its brief *élan*. It was still only half past ten when the first guest looked at her watch, smothered a yawn and remarked in a voice of pure astonishment that she had no idea it was so late.

Clarrie stuck it out to the bitter end, but when she discovered that Toby's presence was due to the fact that he was spending the night with us, and not for the sake of her sparkling eyes or because he wanted to write a play for her, she too lost heart and hauled Steven away.

So, for once, Robin achieved his objective of an early night without even a struggle, although, perversely enough, he did not seem eager to make the most of it.

'After an evening like that, we all need a final drink,' he said, bringing out the brandy glasses. 'I hope you're satisfied, Tessa?'

'No. Why should I be? It was not at all how I'd planned it or how anyone would plan it and I don't see why you should blame me.'

'I daresay I came off better than either of you,' Toby said. 'I dislike parties in any case and, as far as I was concerned, this one was slightly more entertaining than most.'

'That's because you have a warped sense of humour. Personally, I could do without one of the guests practically dropping dead at my feet and another having to be carted home in screaming hysterics. Incidentally, Robin, what could have caused that fit, or whatever it was that Laura had?'

'Do you mean what could have caused it, or what did cause it?'

'I don't know. Aren't they the same thing?'

'It could have happened, I suppose, because she swallowed the wrong way and got a crumb stuck in her gullet – something quite trivial like that. What followed was brought about by a combination of nervous and muscular tension. That could have been the cause, but I can't say whether it was or not.'

'It's very alarming. Almost puts one off eating anything at all, unless you happen to be present to deliver the knock-out blow. Who knows how it might have ended, if she'd been alone? She could have died.'

'No, she couldn't,' Toby said.

'Why not? She'd stopped breathing and that's not something you can afford to do for very long.'

'The point is that it wouldn't have happened, if she'd been alone.'

'Oh, I see! You mean the muscular and nervous tensions wouldn't have functioned without an audience. So it was all our fault? If she'd been alone, she'd have coughed and spluttered a bit and that would have been the end of it?'

'Not at all. If it had been a genuine attack, I imagine the tensions would have been as bad or worse, knowing there was no help at hand. But it wasn't genuine, it was put on, which is another thing you need an audience for.'

'What an extraordinary accusation, Toby! Didn't you see the state she was in?'

'Certainly, I did. It was the wrong state and she turned the wrong colour. She was holding her breath deliberately. I happen to have been unfortunate enough to have witnessed a genuine attack of this sort of thing only a few weeks ago and I know what I am talking about.'

'Really? Who was that?'

'Our very own Dr Macintosh. He was having dinner with me and all at once, for no reason that I could see, he turned stiff and silent as a stone. He was the colour of stone too, whereas Laura was the colour of new brick.'

'What did you do?'

'Nothing. It was as much as I could do to stay where I was and not walk out of the house. Luckily, he was in good hands though, by which I mean his own, of course. He tipped his chair backwards and went crashing down on the floor; and that broke the spell. It broke the chair, too, as it happens, but he was right as rain. Went on with the conversation as though nothing had happened. None of this lying back with eyes closed and needing time to recover.'

'Yes,' Robin agreed, 'it did strike me that she was laying it on a bit thick, specially in view of the effect it was having on Pam. I thought Laura might have made more effort, at least to pretend that there was nothing to worry about. On the other hand, there was some mention of a previous attack and perhaps it takes different people in different ways.'

'I consider it quite likely that she did have a previous attack. That's probably what gave her the idea of staging a repetition tonight. However, she also said that it had been

109

a long time ago and my guess is that it was her memory that let her down. As I discovered from poor Macintosh's experience, it only lasts for about a minute. You could hardly expect the details to remain clear in her mind for twenty or thirty years.'

'But supposing you're right,' I said, 'it still doesn't explain why she did it. I hope you're not going to tell me that she's just as confirmed an exhibitionist as her wretched daughter?'

'Very likely; or else a confirmed hysteric. It would be interesting to know why she did it and it's what made this party a shade less tedious than most.'

'Do you suppose it can have been for the sole purpose of getting Derek off Clarrie's hook? If so, surely she could have found a less drastic solution?'

'It could have been that, all the same,' Robin said. 'As a family, they may lack a talent for acting, but they do seem to have an over-developed sense of drama.'

'And there's something else about the episode which opens up a new field for speculation. When Pam was still moaning and blubbing and Laura was insisting that she needed time to recover before she went home, which personally I accepted as natural at the time, although I daresay Toby's right and she thought this would be expected of her, you remember what happened next? It must have rocked her as much as the rest of us, but I suppose he's become conditioned to flying to the rescue of middle-aged women and may have temporarily confused her with his mother.'

I paused here, waiting for their endorsement or otherwise, and Toby said: 'Have I missed the point, or have you lost it?'

'I didn't realise it needed making. You must have noticed that it was Steven's offer to drive her home which brought about the instant and miraculous recovery. In a trice she was sitting up, brisk and alert and all ready to move off. So why was that? Why in the first place was she so desperately anxious to get away from our lovely party, or so anxious to get Pam away from it that she staged that extravagant drama and was preparing to carry it through to its tiresome end, and why in the second place did she give it all up and return to normal, rather than drive home with Steven?'

'Didn't like the look of him, I daresay, and didn't rate her chances of getting home in one piece very high.'

'You may be right, Toby, but I can't help feeling there might have been more to it than that.'

'Yes, I know,' Robin said, 'and you would cheerfully sit here chewing over it for another hour. Not me, though. I have to be in Birmingham by ten o'clock tomorrow morning and I'm going to bed.'

'Will you need your road map?' I asked, not thinking.

'To get to Birmingham? I hardly think so, unless someone's moved it.'

'Why did you want Robin's road map?' Toby asked, as he and I trailed upstairs a few minutes later.

'For my new hobby. It's called cartography.'

'Yes, so I've heard.'

'I'm learning all sorts of new place names and I religiously look them up on the map and find out how they stand in relation to other places.'

'It sounds most exciting. You must tell me more about it in the morning.'

TWELVE

'How about a trip to the seaside?' I suggested at breakfast.

'Which one?'

'Well, I wasn't proposing to cross the Channel. Brighton might be a good place. You used to love going to Brighton before you got stuck into your rut.'

'Won't it be rather crowded in August?'

'Everywhere's crowded in August, including Roakes Common at present. Besides, we needn't actually mingle. We can look at the sea and snuff up the breezes from our window table in some rarefied restaurant. After that, we'll drive along until we find a nice, secluded beach where you can paddle.'

'You seem to have some very antiquated ideas about the south coast. You would need to drive a hundred miles before you found anything resembling a nice, secluded beach. There are ribbon developments along every inch of it from Folkestone to Bournemouth.'

It is usually best to take one step at a time with Toby, so I did not break it to him that this was precisely why I had chosen it as our destination.

Explanations followed during the journey, however, a move which was forced on me by his incessant complaints about the time it was taking to get there.

'I simply cannot make out where you have been for the last twenty years,' he grumbled, as we joined the queue of cars at a level crossing. 'Don't you realise that they have built all sorts of motorways which take you to Brighton with the speed of light? Nobody with a grain of sense would go through Redhill any more.'

112

'Yes, I do realise. I just wanted to get my bearings.'

'For Brighton?'

'Among other places. Incidentally, there was a turning to Chillingford about five miles back, so I've got that more or less placed in the lay-out. It was getting a bit late to make a detour then, if we're to be in time for that lunch we've promised ourselves, but we might take it in on our way home.'

'What a frightful idea! May I ask what other horrors you have in store?'

'Only one other that really matters, but it may take time and involve a modicum of subterfuge.'

'That would not surprise me. Does it have anything to do with that ghastly wig you're wearing?'

'It is rather hideous, I admit, but it has to be red, you see. That's the one thing most people notice right away and remember ever afterwards. When I'm wearing my outsize sunglasses too, which I fully intend to do, so it's lucky there's plenty of glare, I hope to be practically unrecognisable.'

'To whom?'

'Anyone who might conceivably have seen me on stage or screen, or heard about me from some spy. I thought you could pretend to be my stepbrother. That should put them even further off the scent because, if there's one thing my public does know about me, it is that I haven't got a stepbrother.'

'And, after all that, could you please explain who it is you expect to be fooling with this nonsense?'

'Oh, good! Here comes the train at last. Now perhaps we can move.'

'It may be all nonsense,' I admitted when we had done so, 'and perhaps it won't lead to anything, but I hate unfinished business and I thought I'd have one last shot at solving some of these riddles.'

'And which one have you earmarked for today?'

113

'Well, it's like this, you see, Toby. I've met almost all the living characters in this drama, which has now been rumbling on for about fifty years, but there are two omissions. One is Dodie, who is now plastered in Denmark and will have to wait. The other, who I'd been afraid would remain for ever inaccessible, is Tom.'

'Who's he?'

'Tom Lampeter, Laura's brother and the only male, so far as is known, of the Seymour issue. He may have no part to play at all, he may not even know that Baba is writing a book which will contain documented proof that his mother was a cheat and a harlot and that he is not Sheridan's son, after all. On the other hand, perhaps he does know, in which case I would guess that he is none too pleased about it. In fact, he would probably view it with even less favour than the rest of them.'

'Why?'

'Because I suspect that he is already an embittered man. Sheridan left him a lot of money, you know, and he lost every penny financing his own plays, if you can believe such a thing?'

'Only with immense difficulty.'

'They were all utter flops, but that didn't deter him, so he must have believed in them himself. Knowing that type of swollen-headed imbecile, I expect he put their failure down to bad casting, spiteful critics, or any old reason except the true one. So I imagine it might really destroy his last pathetic illusions to discover that he had no talent, for the very obvious reason that there wasn't a drop of Seymour blood in his veins.'

'Yes, indeed, but would you mind explaining what all this has to do with our spending the day in Brighton?'

'It's probably a fifty-to-one shot, but it happens to be a name that has cropped up more than once just lately and each time linked in some way with the Seymour/Lampeter saga. When Derek first told me about his wife's family he

114

said that her uncle Tom had joined some evangelical sect who were based near Brighton. That made no impression at the time, but for some reason the memory was stirred when Robin was telling me about the routes this unknown woman who impersonated Dodie Watson might have taken to get to Mallings. Thinking it over afterwards, I remembered that he'd said that from Redhill, which is the nearest mainline junction, there are branch lines to various places along the coast to the east and west of Brighton. So that was the second time it had come up.'

'Personally, I find the link fragile, to say the least.'

'So did I at that stage, but hang on a minute because last night, when I was talking to Laura, she mentioned something which set the same wheels turning again. That was before she had her funny turn and, if your theory about that is true, it could have been what brought it on.'

'What could? I have lost the thread again.'

'A little throw-away remark, which on reflection she may have wished unsaid. I was trying to draw her out, which was uphill work, and one of the subjects I ploughed into was her stay in the country. She said it wasn't real country, just a nasty little bungalow town on the south coast.'

'And not far from Brighton?'

'Better than that. She said it was called Beachclyffe. Last night, after you'd both gone to bed, I looked it up on Robin's map and guess what? It's about midway between Brighton and Bognor. As I say, it's just possible that was her reason for staging the attack. She wanted to avoid the risk of being needled into any further indiscretions. She'd have heard by then from Angie, if not from Derek, that I've taken it on myself to delve about in their family affairs, to find a way to stop Baba rocking their boats, but who's to say how far she trusts me? Furthermore, she had no way of telling whose side Steven was on and it was his offer to drive her home, you remember, which brought

115

about an instant recovery.'

'But suppose she had been staying with her brother, what's wrong with that? And why the hell should she mind your knowing?'

'Who can say? But when I invented a pretext to find out the name of the people she'd been staying with, she shut up like a clam and more or less indicated that I might try minding my own business. So either she's very secretive by nature or else she has something to hide, in which case I thought it might be amusing to find out what it is.'

'Oh, I see! Such as she and her brother having set fire to a house under the mistaken impression that their half-sister was in residence?'

'That would do nicely. No need to remind you that this sojourn at the seaside did coincide with the fire at Mallings.'

'So what are you proposing to do? Wander up and down Beachclyffe, knocking on every door to enquire whether Mr Thomas Lampeter is at home? Or perhaps you mean to seek out the headquarters of the evangelist group and get his address from them? What do they call themselves, by the way?'

'I haven't the faintest idea.'

'Doesn't that pose a problem?'

'Not at all. It may end with our being shown over half a dozen fairly unattractive houses, but that is bound to provide insights and entertainment of a kind and none of them is likely to be large, so it shouldn't take long.'

'Now what are you talking about, I wonder?'

'The fact that most of the obstacles have already been smoothed away by something else which came out of my conversation with Laura. She said the owners hadn't bothered to keep up the garden because they were hoping to sell the place.'

'Can it be that you mean to call at all the local estate agents and enquire whether they have a property on their books in the name of Lampeter?'

'No, I don't think we want to be quite so open about it as that and anyway we don't know for certain that he still uses that name. My idea was to drive around, making a note of bungalows with a For Sale board outside, eliminating the non-starters and then taking the rest in order of merit.'

'What does merit mean?'

'Well, for a start, it has to be modern and packed in among a lot of others of the same ilk. It must have a small, neglected garden and be at least one mile from the sea. That should whittle it down enough to complete the job in a couple of hours, at the outside.'

'And, having whittled, what then?'

'Oh, do stop niggling, Toby. They're not likely to be the sort of places that can only be viewed by appointment, so why don't we just say that we happened to be passing and wondered if we might take a look round? That's another reason why it might be a good idea if you were my stepbrother. You haven't got a wife, you see, so you've brought me along to look at things from a woman's angle. If the owners are not at home, of course, we shall have to fall back on the agent, but in either event our story will be the same. Are you game?'

'Oh, I suppose so, though I must confess that the only part I care for in this role in which I've been cast is not having a wife. I'm not at all sure that I see myself as a stepbrother who would contemplate living in the sort of place you have described. However, I have no doubt that you will do the talking for both of us, so there'll be no need to wear myself out trying to make it convincing.'

I shall skate rapidly over the first part of our afternoon's adventures, because failure is best forgotten and nothing turned out as I had hoped. For one thing, Beachclyffe did not fit in with my preconceived notion of how it would look. It covered a much bigger area and its buildings seemed to have been thrown up in such a hurry as to deprive it of any form or pattern in which to carry out our research on a scientific basis. We found only two houses which fitted the bill in all respects, but the annoying part was that for each of those we may have missed half a dozen others by going round in circles. At one point we found ourselves driving down the same depressing little mud road for the second time in ten minutes, when it should by rights have been at least half a mile away.

Toby by this time was wavering between pleasure at being able to point out the absurdity of my optimism and the fear of overdoing it, lest, taunted into defiance, I should insist on carrying on until the stars appeared in the sky.

In fact, I was nearer to capitulation than he had realised and offered a compromise.

'Okay, Toby, indulge me for just five more minutes. Let us go back to Holmbushe, which as we now know must be in the road parallel to this one. It is not so mean and scruffy-looking as Laura's description had prepared me for, but at least it's for sale and the lawn looks like a daisy field.'

'And that will really be the last?'

'Word of honour. If we draw a blank there I'll drive straight up to the main road and all the way back to Beacon Square, without a single stop.'

The doorbell was answered as the last chime died away, which I took to be a good omen, and the man who answered it provided further crumbs of encouragement. He was tall, thin and stooping, with wispy straggling hair and a matching beard. This, combined with the fact that the interior was dingy and poorly lighted and I still had my sunglasses on, made it difficult to judge whether he bore any resemblance to known members of the Seymour/ Latimer clan. He was the right age group, though, and he had the right sort of nervous and defeated manner.

'Oh. .. er ... are you looking for someone?' he asked, backing away as he spoke.

'Not exactly,' I replied, embarking on the prepared speech for the third time. 'My name is Price, by the way, and this is my stepbrother. He's looking for a little holiday cottage, not too far from the sea. We've seen round one or two places, but nothing we liked, and when we saw the board outside we wondered if you'd mind showing us over. If it's not inconvenient, that is.'

'It's not inconvenient,' he replied in a sad voice, 'but I'm afraid you'll be wasting your time. I doubt if it'll suit you. Still, come inside, if you'd like to.'

He led us through the narrow, cramped little hall and then into a small, square room overlooking the daisy field, where he remained standing just inside the door.

Among other cheap-looking furniture it contained two armchairs, with a table between them laid for tea, and leaning back in one of them was a woman who was also tall and thin, with wispy, colourless hair.

'We saw your car go by twice,' she said in an amused and painfully familiar drawl, 'and we wondered how long it would take you to find us.'

'Oh, hello!' I said, removing the sunglasses and trying not to sound as silly as I felt. 'Fancy seeing you! I expect you've met Angie Petworth, haven't you, Toby?'

'How did you know it was us?' I asked a few minutes later.

'Recognised your car. It was parked outside the shop for several hours, if you remember, and I had plenty of time to stop and stare while you were making up your mind.'

'All the same, it was clever of you,' Toby said. 'It is quite a popular model, I understand.'

'I expect the truth is,' I suggested, 'that you were expecting us?'

'Not both of you and not so soon, I admit. So few cars venture down this road, though, that it becomes noticeable when the same one passes twice in half an hour.'

'Did Laura warn you that I might be coming?'

'Would you like some tea?' Tom asked in his mild and diffident way. 'I was just about to make it.'

'You would be quite safe in saying yes,' Angie assured us. 'He is far more domesticated than I am and he makes better tea, so they tell me.'

'I am feeling domesticated myself,' Toby informed us, 'so I shall accompany him, if I may? And perhaps you would also be so kind as to direct me to the bathroom? Not that I wish to inspect it with a view to buying your house, you understand?'

When they had both gone I repeated my question:

'Did Laura warn you?'

'Much too strong a word. She telephoned last night and told Tom there was a possibility that you might get in touch with him. It was after she got home from your party and she was rather worried that she might have let him in for something. That probably sounds silly to you, but he is very shy and awkward with strangers and the mere thought of being confronted by one is enough to throw him into a panic. So he immediately applied to me for advice, which is something he has been in the habit of doing since he was five years old.'

'And you immediately got in the car and drove down here to hold his hand?'

'Which is something I've been in the habit of doing since I was twelve. Not that it was any great inconvenience this time. Mondays are usually slack at the shop and I often give myself the day off.'

'It's odd, though, because I got the impression that he had dropped out of your lives since he fell on hard times?'

'And so he did, for almost ten years, which was as long as his marriage lasted. His wife didn't approve of us and our material values. To be fair, she did make one effort, early on, to extend the olive branch by offering Baba the

120

chance to part with some of her money, but when that failed her disapproval increased and she succeeded in turning Tom against the lot of us.'

'What happened to her!'

'Beryl? Oh, she died about two years ago. Heart attack, they said it was. Brought on by rage and frustration, I shouldn't wonder.'

I did not comment and Angie said, 'Aren't you going to ask me what had enraged and frustrated her?'

'I thought I'd better not. It's really no business of mine.'

'True, but it might amuse you. She'd already left him, you see, a few months before she had the heart attack. She didn't run off with another man, or for any of the usual reasons, though, but because she'd lost her faith.'

'And that annoyed her?'

'Very much. Silly woman! She'd have done better to let Tom go his own way and make the best of it. She was an exceptionally unattractive woman, and bossy with it, so her life can't have been much fun for those few months. And none of it had ever bothered Tom. He's been surrounded by bossy women all his life and not all of them have been attractive. The only time he struck out on his own and ignored our advice it ended so disastrously that he hasn't tried it again.'

'How did he and Beryl meet?'

'She was a nurse at the hospital where he worked as an ambulance driver. Recognising a lost and lonely soul when she saw one, she invited him to one of her prayer meetings and in no time at all he'd been converted. In next to no time at all they were married. When she walked out on him he became lost and lonely again and threw himself back on the bossy sisters.'

'I still don't understand why she had to leave him. As you say, why not just have stayed at home and let him go and pray on his own?'

'Tom says it was because she was too fine a person to

121

live a lie, but then, being incorruptible himself, he takes a more charitable view than the rest of us. Personally, I saw it as a gamble which didn't come off.'

'What was she gambling on?'

'Her power over him. In other words, that when she renounced her faith he would follow suit and obediently take up his old life again at the point where it was before she met him. But he wasn't having any. She had done her work too well. Better, I imagine, than her voices had foretold. He has now become quite the little guru, revered by all the faithful and much in demand by the followers who travel from miles around to sit at his feet. Poor, misguided Tom, how little they know! But he revels in it, of course, and it would have taken more than Beryl's nagging to sway him from the straight and narrow path now.'

'Why did she want him to? I gather he wasn't particularly successful in his early life?'

'No, but at least he had powerful and affluent connections, specially since my father's plays had started coming back into fashion. I think she saw Tom's conversion as a passport to marriage and very likely she had the idea all along that it might eventually include a visa allowing her to enter that world as his wife. When it didn't come off, I imagine she saw his religious beliefs as the main obstacle and she tried to blackmail him into renouncing them by threatening to leave him.'

'But he called her bluff? Didn't he feel guilty and remorseful about it when she died?'

'Not so far, but it's too soon to tell. That may come later, of course.'

'Oh, but surely . . .?'

'No, what I mean is that perhaps the day will come when some other viper decides to take him on, someone very like Beryl, and he'll fall for it again and be back where he started. We can't always be around to protect him.'

122

At this point the subject of our conversation entered the room, carrying the tea tray, which he deposited on the table beside Angie and then retired to a chair in the remotest corner of the room. He was followed by Toby, looking unexpectedly cheerful.

'Tom and I have been having an interesting discussion about plays,' he announced. 'He has given me some most original and ingenious plot lines. I am thinking of asking him to collaborate with me on writing one of them.'

'That's a splendid idea,' I told him. 'In that way he could do all the hard work and you could add the flourishes. Angie and I have had an interesting discussion too. In fact, it's not quite finished yet because I have one more question which got lost among all the others. I hope you won't mind my asking it now, Angie?'

'No, not at all. I am getting accustomed.'

'Then could you please explain why Laura made such a secret of the fact that she came down here to spend a few days with her brother and why she was so anxious to prevent my finding out?'

'Ah well, that is the one we were expecting and we've been debating how to answer it ever since we saw your car go by. What do you say, Tom? Shall we own up?'

'That's for you to decide,' he replied predictably enough, from his corner.

'I think we should really. We've gone in too deep to withdraw now. Very well, you shall have the full story and perhaps it will provide Toby with a few more original and ingenious plot lines.'

'It started as a harmless prank,' she began, 'the sort of trick we used to play on each other as children. Four of us would gang up against another who needed taking down a peg.'

'Four?' I enquired.

'Yes, I exclude Tom. He was the baby, you see, years younger than the rest of us and we'd more or less grown out of the pranky stage by the time he was of an age to take part. Besides, I doubt if he'd have been much of an asset. He lacks the malicious streak which was always so essential. I think that's why my mother doted on him so much. In some peculiar way, she felt he was the one she had most in common with.'

'I take it that Baba was usually the victim, then as now?'

'Oh, absolutely! Looking back, I can see that jealousy probably had a lot to do with it. She was so gorgeous looking that everyone fell for her the minute they set eyes on her. They fell for all her lies and boasting too and by the time she was in her teens she'd become unbearably cocky and conceited. She still is, of course, and when Dodie told us about two years ago that she was writing her autobiography we thought how typical of Baba to imagine that her life story could have the faintest interest for anyone except herself. We weren't particularly bothered, though. We knew it would be crammed with untruths and exaggerations and self-praise, but in those days it never occurred to us that she could get away with it and that anyone would be potty enough to publish the damn thing.'

'When did it begin to dawn on you?'

'Not for months and then only gradually. Dodie kept us informed of every move, of course, and after a while the word began to get around about Baba and her scandalous memoirs, but we still felt safe. Sooner or later, we said, she'd become bored and switch her creative talent to some other project.'

'You evidently underrated her this time, though.'

'Yes, we did. I don't remember exactly when the change set in, but it must have been six or eight months ago. Nor do I know exactly who it is we have to thank for it. Dodie told us that some literary agent had entered the fray and taken on the Svengali role just when Baba was beginning to flag. He not only introduced her to one or two publishers, for whom she gave lavish and swanky dinner parties, but for some reason best known to himself he was supervising work on the book as well. Apparently, they spent hours together every week, with the tape recorder going full blast. But Baba was being very cagey about this miracle man and not even Dodie had been allowed to meet him. From our point of view he was bad news, because from the bits she had typed herself, before Baba hired a professional secretary, instead of trying to tone down the lies and absurdities, he was egging her on to even worse excesses. It must have been heady wine for her and that's when we really started to worry; Laura, in particular.'

'Why in particular?'

'Because she's much more up in the writing and publishing game than the rest of us and it was her opinion that this scamp wasn't giving out his time and energy just to flatter a vain and silly woman, or because he was impressed by her background and title. The chances were that he really had got some slightly raffish publisher lined up and that, as her co-author, there would be quite a lot in it for him, if he could persuade Baba to come up with enough lurid scandals in high places. So that was when we hatched our plot.'

'Which had something to do with those mysterious love letters, I take it?'

'Quite right, it had everything to do with them.'

'And whose idea was it?'

'Laura's. She was always the clever one, wasn't she, Tom? Just as Baba was the beauty and you were the good one.'

'That's rubbish, you know, dear, and I think we ought to make it clear that Laura had nothing to do with carrying it out.'

These were the first words that Tom had uttered since

the story began and I noticed that most of the time he sat with his hand covering the lower part of his face, as though forcibly to prevent himself from joining in. His eyes were never still, though, and they had a strange, rather alarming glint in them, quite in keeping with the manic visionary of Angie's description.

'Yes, you're right,' she said now. 'Having planted her seed, Laura retired to a quieter part of the garden. I think she was afraid that, if the truth ever came out, it would rebound on her and she wanted to protect her own hard-won reputation.'

'But she knew what was going on?'

'Dodie saw to that, whether she liked it or not. My sister Dodie spends half her life on the telephone and no detail goes unrecorded.'

'But what exactly was going on?' Toby asked. 'I do think it's time somebody told me.'

Angie glanced enquiringly at Tom, who inclined his head slightly, and then she said, 'If you have the patience to listen, but I should warn you that it was rather an elaborate hoax, as they usually were, and you will need to hear it all if you are to understand why it misfired, to use a really terrible pun, and why we now find ourselves in something of a fix.'

'Which is also why you have decided to break the silence?' I suggested. 'Being in something of a fix, you could use a helping hand?'

'No, not necessarily, but it wouldn't surprise me if you'd guessed part of the story already. It would be a pity if you got it right, all except for the climax. It started, as you say, with the idea of those bogus letters. Laura's contention was that, now that this new menace had appeared on the scene, just lying low and hoping for the best would be futile. We could no longer shut our eyes to the fact that the book, in some form or other, was going to get written and very likely published and some pretty

126

sensational, defamatory and embarrassing material it was bound to contain. Suing for libel would be out of the question. It would be a free gift of exactly the kind of publicity they were both hoping for. So the only answer was to beat her at her own game and provide her with the scoop to make her dreams come true, something so irresistible that she would be tempted to be more than usually careless about checking the facts. Then, if the day came when we heard that she had signed a contract and everything was chugging along at the printers, we'd send an anonymous tip-off to the publishers, enclosing a copy of one of the forgeries Baba had included in her manuscript. We thought that would do the trick.'

'I am sure you were right,' I admitted. 'Which one of you did the forging?'

'Tom.'

'That must have taken a lot of skill and practice, surely, even taking into account Baba's carelessness?'

I had addressed this question directly to Tom, who now sat with his elbows on his knees and his face cupped in his hands.

'No, not a lot,' he replied in his sad, gentle voice, which was so much at odds with the fanatical eyes. 'I started imitating my father's handwriting when I was a boy. It was all part of the campaign to turn myself into a carbon copy of him, so it came quite naturally.'

'And we'd kept some of the letters he'd written to us during his lifetime,' Angie explained. 'I suppose we'd always nursed faint hopes that one day he'd have a revival and we'd make our fortunes when they came up for sale at Sotheby's. So we had plenty of examples to draw on for his style and favourite expressions, not to mention misspellings. For the purpose of our forgeries, we used the period when I was at a boarding school, or being finished abroad, as they used to call it. So I was more or less of an age with our fictitious heroine and could even reproduce

127

some of the terms in which she'd have written back. I told you this was a very elaborate plan.'

'And I am filled with admiration,' Toby confessed. 'Not only for your being so thorough, but for going to all that trouble simply to save one sister from embarrassment and humiliation at the hands of another.'

'I am afraid you over-estimate us. It wasn't only Laura we were worried about. Baba's main object was to destroy Kitty Lampeter's reputation and the rest of us had all been devoted to Kitty. Besides, I can't believe it would have stopped there. If I know Baba, she wouldn't have spared my mother either and, speaking for myself, there are one or two episodes in my past that I shouldn't much enjoy having dragged out and paraded in public. No, there was a lot more at stake than poor Laura's susceptibilities. Isn't that right, Tom?'

'So what was the next move?' I asked, when Tom had responded with his silent and obedient nod. 'After the letters had been written, tied up in blue ribbon and left to moulder in the dust for a bit? Renting some suitable premises to discover them in, presumably?'

'Which took longer than we'd bargained for. There were so many requirements.'

'Like?'

'Well, the location wasn't particularly important, so long as it was within fairly easy reach of London and of course it had to be somewhere where none of us ran any risk of being recognised. Expense was a limitation too, although not a serious one, since in our more light-hearted moments we were hoping to get our hands on quite a whack of Baba's ill-gotten gains to reward us for all our trouble. In a general way, we set out to find something modest, with obvious disadvantages for the average tenant, reasonably isolated from curious neighbours, but not so much so that the comings and goings of an ordinary looking middle-aged woman would pass completely unnoticed. In other words, where we could fade naturally into the background. It was several months before we finally came across this nasty little Victorian villa at Mallings. It had been lived in for about fifteen years by an elderly couple of slender means, who had made no improvements whatever. The plumbing was archaic and, as we all now know so well, the electric wiring was in a sorry state too and it had been empty for almost a year. When the old man died his widow stayed on for a bit and on her death it passed to a married niece, who lives in Harrogate and had been trying to get it off her hands ever since. She was willing to rent it, with the existing furniture, subject to a month's notice, if a prospective buyer should turn up. The widow had been called Elizabeth, so that became the name of our father's light of love.'

'And what name did you use when you wrote to Baba to inform her of your great discovery?' I asked.

'The niece's, of course. No mention of Harrogate, naturally, and we used a box number in Chillingford, on the grounds that the negotiations were being kept secret from her husband.'

'All the same, wasn't it rather risky to rent the house in Dodie's name?'

'Not really. As a short term tenant, her name wouldn't appear on any register or telephone directory.'

'I was only thinking that when her lovely dream turned into a nightmare, Baba might have got her bloodhounds on the trail of whoever it was who had played this fiendish trick on her and their first move, surely, would have been to make enquiries locally? How about those estate agents, for a start?'

'Well, it wouldn't have mattered much at that stage, would it? The game would have been over by then and we should have won it. There was nothing Baba could have done about it, without making herself look a bigger fool than ever. Naturally, though, we didn't want anything like that to happen before we were ready to move in for the kill, so we did take a few precautions. Or rather, we tried to tie it up in so many knots that it could never be unravelled.'

'How did you do that?'

'We paid the rent in advance, in cash, and we used Dodie's bank as a reference, but the agents never saw her and they wouldn't have recognised the real Dodie's photograph. What they saw was another middle-aged woman of no particular distinction, but with quite different features and hair. Dodie takes after her father, you see, and I don't.'

'Yes, I do see. How very crafty!'

'Wasn't it? I think we'd have got away with it too, if it hadn't been for this blasted fire. At any rate, I haven't had a policeman knocking on my door to ask whether I've been impersonating any of my sisters lately.'

'Not so far,' Toby remarked, 'but there may be changes on the way and I feel it is very trusting of you to confess all this to Tessa, knowing where her loyalties lie.'

'I think she'd guessed a good bit of it already and, besides, what can it matter now? We have nothing left to lose, the letters we toiled over for so many weeks have presumably gone up in smoke and I refuse to believe that we've broken any law. So far as I am concerned, they can ask as many questions as they please and I should simply say that I looked at some houses for my sister, mainly because she has more faith in my judgement than her own, which happens to be true.'

I was about to point to one important omission in this summing up of the situation, but Toby got there first:

'It seems to me that you have overlooked something.'

'Oh? Do tell me!'

'I may be wrong, of course, but it occurs to me that one of the questions you might be asked will have something to do with the woman who was burnt to death.'

Angie was looking amused, which was a bad sign.

'In that case, I should have no alternative but to answer them truthfully, should I?'

'And what would you tell them?'

'That we have no more idea than they have who she was.'

'Oh, I see! And you think that will be the end of it? No more questions?'

'Dozens, I daresay, but all to no purpose. She was obviously someone who had no business to be there, since she certainly didn't ask our permission, but that's about all I can say.'

'And you weren't there yourself that evening?'

'No, we scarcely ever went near the place at night, except in the very early days, to establish what you might call an *acte de presence*.'

'I suppose you could prove that, if necessary?' I asked.

'Curiously enough, I do believe we could. We've had plenty of time to talk things over, we merry band of hoaxers, and we've discovered that all three of us were otherwise engaged that evening. I exclude Dodie, of course, because she was in Denmark. Would you like to hear about the rest of us?'

Without waiting for an answer, she went on, 'I am sure you would, so I shall tell you. I was at home in my flat in Pinbury and, if proof were needed, they could have it. I went down to the local pub just before they closed because I was running out of cigarettes and, as you know, they don't open till twelve on Sundays. Nothing particularly unusual about that. For some strange reason, I invariably do run out of cigarettes on Saturday evening, after the shops are shut. As you may also know, it takes a minimum of four hours to drive from there to the outskirts of Redhill.'

'How about the other two?'

131

'They were together, which wraps it all up rather neatly. Laura had driven Dodie to Gatwick Airport the day before and she came on here to spend a few days with Tom, who'd had a bad cold and is quite incapable of looking after himself. At about ten o'clock the telephone rang. Tom answered it and passed it over to Laura. It was Pam, in an advanced state of hysteria because she thought she was having contraction pains. Laura didn't take it seriously, she'd heard it all before. She told Pam what to do and then she got Derek on the line and told him what to do and said she'd ring back in the morning. Some time after midnight, long after they'd both gone to bed, it rang again and the same pattern was repeated. Tom went downstairs to answer it and it was Pam again, demanding to speak to Laura. He tried to explain that she was in bed and asleep, but Pam insisted, so he padded upstairs, called Laura, who came down and Pam told her that the nasty pains had gone away and she needn't lie awake worrying, after all. They both cursed her at the time, needless to say, but perhaps it will turn out that she did the right thing, for once in her life.'

'Yes, it sounds as though she did. All the same, Angie, I suppose they might get to hear about those famous letters and perhaps even put two and two together. You wouldn't be able to deny you'd sent them and that therefore one of you was the mysterious tenant of Fairview, Mallings, near Chillingford.'

'What if they did? As I've said before, we've committed no crime and no money has changed hands. The worst that could happen would be another victory for Baba. It would almost make up to her for the loss of her beloved letters, if we could be shown up in such a bad light. And just for the record, I'd like to point out that, after all our hard work and careful organisation, we're hardly likely to have found such a difficult, complicated and dangerous way of destroying them as to burn the house down. There

132

must be easier ways and, if you really mean to pursue this any further, I'll give you a word of advice.'

'I'm not sure that I do, but go ahead, anyway.'

'I've told you before that, personally, I mean to keep out of it and I shouldn't even mention this to the police, if they were ever to seek my views on the subject and, in any case, as far as I can see, there's nothing whatever they or anyone else can do about it. However, if you're interested, I can tell you exactly who the woman was who was killed in the fire.'

'Can you really, Angie? My word, that is a surprise!'

'It shouldn't be. Obviously, Baba had been tipped off, or for some other reason had got the wind up about the letters being bogus. Either that, or more likely still, knowing her, she was beginning to resent having to pay out such a lot of money for them. Whichever it was, her first move would have been to try and get her hands on them without the owner's knowing and the second would have been to hire some bent and scruffy private detective to do the job for her. It wouldn't have been the first time, I assure you. Equally obviously, they would have used the services of a middle-aged, nondescript female as their operative. I imagine that one of the places she'd have looked in would have been the attic. She wouldn't have found them there, as it happens, but there was plenty of stuff stored up there, including trunks and packing cases filled with junk, and the search could have taken her several hours. Presumably, the fire started while she was up there and had got a proper hold by the time she tried to come down. No one heard her screams, the staircase was burning and there is no telephone upstairs. End of story. How about some more tea? I'm afraid we can't offer you anything stronger. It's against Tom's principles.'

133

THIRTEEN

Ellen was typing when I called at her flat to report on our day at the seaside. It was an unusual-looking page because each line was the length of exactly four letters, so most of the words started on one line and finished on the one below and several had three all to themselves.

'It's my new electronic typewriter,' she explained. 'Jeremy gave it to me and I have a sneaking suspicion that it was only because his secretary has refused to touch it. I've pressed every knob in sight and it doesn't make the slightest difference. After four taps it goes smartly back to the margin again. Why should that be, do you suppose?'

'Simple,' I replied, 'there was a mix-up at the works and this one landed on the wrong conveyor belt. It has the export keyboard and home market mechanism. No doubt you would find that four spaces is just right for one Japanese character.'

'Oh well, that's no good, then. Come on, let's go into the other room and have some coffee while you tell me all the news.'

'Dodie's back,' she announced, when I had done so, 'did you know?'

'Yes, Robin told me.'

'Do you still want to meet her?'

'Not much point now, do you think? Whether Angie's theory is right or not, and I daresay it is, my reasons for getting mixed up with that tiresome family no longer exist. My object was simply to help Laura out of a fix, in order to calm down Pam, which would have pleased Derek and ultimately Robin would have benefited. None

134

of them needs my help now that the letters have been destroyed and if they find something else to get ruffled about they must sort it out for themselves. I start work next week and, in the meantime, I've still got some strawberries to grapple with.'

'Dodie wants to meet you,' Ellen said.

'Does she? How do you know?'

'She rang up this morning. Said she'd found a note on her message pad that I'd been trying to get in touch with her. That was ages ago, of course, before we knew she'd gone abroad.'

'So?'

'So, naturally, she wanted to know why I'd tried to get in touch.'

'What did you tell her?'

'I wasn't ready for it, you see, so I said the first thing that came into my head.'

'Which, knowing you, was the truth?'

'Well, yes, I'm afraid so, Tessa. No details, you know, I simply said I'd been having a few people to lunch. You were coming and I'd hoped she would too.'

'And she said she was sorry to have missed it and hoped you'd invite her some other time when I was going to be there again?'

'Her exact words.'

'Probably just being polite.'

'I'm not sure about that. She didn't just throw it out in a glib sort of way. That's not her style, for one thing. She doesn't go in for sugary insincerities like Baba. And, in fact, she laid it on quite thick. About how much she admired you and what fun it would have been to meet you and so forth. She's fairly naive, you know.'

'Quite so.'

'No offence. It's just that, although she's spent her whole life on the fringes of the theatre, she's still stage-struck. All the same, from the way she was going

135

on, I do think there was more to it than that and she really had some special reason for wanting to meet you.'

'And what could that have been, do you suppose?'

'I don't know, except that she also harped a good bit on the fact that ever since she got back from Denmark the police have been on at her about this woman who'd been impersonating her and how it was really getting her down.'

'That wouldn't necessarily have anything to do with this sudden urge to meet me. Or would it?'

'Well. . .now that you've told me about walking into the lion's den at Beachclyffe, I was wondering if Angie might possibly have put her up to it?'

'I hardly think so. Angie took the attitude that once again Baba had won hands down, virtually got away with murder in the process and there was nothing whatever that anyone could do about it. However, perhaps that was just thrown out as a challenge and she was hoping I'd bestir myself to prove her wrong.'

'And has now enlisted Dodie's help in keeping you interested and on your toes?'

'In which case, Ellen, I feel quite tempted to fall in with their crafty little plot.'

'Do you? Why?'

'Because it would indicate that everything Angie told us during that bizarre session at Beachclyffe was true and not just a whitewashed version she and Tom had patched up for my benefit. Otherwise, the last thing she'd want would be to have me prowling around and digging out more facts. She certainly wouldn't have encouraged Dodie to get in touch with me and start everything up again.'

'So you've changed your mind about not wanting to meet her?'

'I have no particular objection, so long as it fell out like that, without any pushing and persuasion.'

'Oh no, none of that. I did mention that, if she was

really so keen to meet you, it would have to be soon because you were starting rehearsals in just over a week.'

'And?'

'She said she'd be free on Thursday and Friday of this week and pretty well every day of the one after. Friday would be all right for me too, so if you like I'll call her back this evening and confirm it.'

'Really, Ellen, it begins to sound as though all my weighing up of the pros and cons has been rather a waste of time. Am I really so transparent?'

'No, of course you're not.'

'I don't believe you, but never mind. It might be interesting to meet Dodie and at least it will complete the last bit of tidying up before my retirement. She is the only one of the Seymour descendants who is still just a name to me. On Friday I shall be able to get her face into the picture and have it framed as a souvenir.'

Ellen had been quick off the mark, but not quick enough because by Friday morning, the day of her lunch party, Dodie was already dead.

Robin brought the news when he came home from work on Thursday evening.

'When?' I asked, coming out of a stunned silence.

'This afternoon. In hospital, or on her way there by ambulance.'

'What was it? An overdose?'

'Underdose might be a better description. She'd gone into a deep coma and died before they could give her the treatment which, even at that stage, might have brought her out of it. She was diabetic, it seems.'

'Yes, I remember hearing that. It must have been Aunt Em who told me. How long had she been in her coma?'

'Hard to say, but not less than twelve hours and it could have been much more. She hadn't been seen or heard from since yesterday morning.'

137

'Who eventually found her?'

'A neighbour, from a flat on the same floor. She and Dodie had a reciprocal arrangement about keeping an eye on things when one or other of them was away and she had the front door key.'

'Yes, I've heard about her too. What alerted her this time? More milk bottles?'

'No, newspapers. They were still on the mat outside at lunch time yesterday. She didn't worry because Dodie was well known for being vague and forgetful, but this morning when she went out they were still there and with a new lot piled on top of them. At which point, having rung the bell and got no response, she let herself in.'

'And that tells you something too, doesn't it?'

'About neighbours?'

'No, about Dodie Watson. If anyone has got the idea that she committed suicide, they might as well forget it. Obviously, she had stopped the papers before she went to Denmark and she'd hardly have gone to all the trouble of re-ordering them when she got back if she had no intention of reading them. And, anyway, if she did mean to commit suicide, why not have done so in Denmark and saved herself all the nerve-racking hassle and interrogation when she got back?'

'I suppose it might have been the hassle and interrogation which brought her to the pitch, but it's too early for speculations of that kind. We shall have to wait for the post mortem.'

'When will you hear?'

'Tomorrow, I suppose. Remind me to let you know when I come home.'

'Oh, I will. You may depend on it.'

138

Before going to bed that evening, I telephoned Ellen to pass on the news, but she'd already heard it.

'How come?' I asked. 'It wasn't in the evening paper.'

'Peregrine told me. You know, Baba's son. Jeremy and I had been invited to dine there next week, before he goes back to America, and he rang up to say it was off.'

'Did he tell you how his mother was taking this latest catastrophe?'

'Relatively calmly, I gather. She's making a muted drama out of it, instead of the full, orchestrated, three-act variety. Will you come to lunch on your own tomorrow?'

'No, I think not, thank you, Ellen. I've got a rehearsal call on Tuesday morning. Not wishing to be ungracious, you know, but since I'm never going to know now why Dodie was so anxious to meet me, I think it's time to forget about it and concentrate on my lines.'

'Okay, just as you like. Do you suppose one of them killed her?'

'Almost certainly,' I replied without hesitation, or much thought either, since this was an idea which had only been hovering beneath the surface, under layers of other conjectures and speculations.

'Which one?'

'Baba, presumably, or one of her agents. Perhaps that's why she's now lying low and cancelling dinner parties. Coming on top of everything else, it would really be stretching coincidence a bit far, don't you think, to imagine her death was due simply to carelessness?'

'I don't know, she was very vague and impractical and,

as you say, Tessa, coming on top of everything else, what motive could there have been for wanting her out of the way now? Baba's precious letters have blown up in her face. She may not realise they were only a trick, but she must know that they no longer exist, so what threat could Dodie pose for her?'

'Unless she had realised, after she got home, that she was the intended victim of the fire, that Baba was behind it and she had every intention of passing on the news to you and me? Why not? It hangs together, after a fashion. And the annoying part is that, if it's true, dear old Baba has every chance of getting away with it.'

Ellen gave such a deep sigh that I could hear it humming down the wires.

'Honestly, Tess, I don't know how you can bear to give it up and retire now, just when everything's building up again. How will you be able to concentrate on made-up characters and situations when you've got all this real life banging on your door?'

'I daresay it won't be easy, but imaginary characters and situations are the mainstay of my existence and I don't intend to sacrifice them for silly old real life. When it comes to a choice between them, truth and justice must struggle on without me.'

'Fine talk', as Robin says, but just as insubstantial, when it came to the point, as such talk usually is.

Even as I re-read the script on Friday morning, studied the schedule and made a stab at memorising my lines for the opening sequence, one part of my mind kept slipping away to frolic among the participants of that other drama which had claimed so much of my attention during the preceding weeks.

Deluding myself that concentration would come more easily if my hands had some more constructive occupation than stubbing out half-smoked cigarettes, I picked up the now crumpled square of tapestry and had a go at that.

All it did, though, was to revive memories of Aunt Em and her reminiscences of the Seymour girls when young and when their mother was still alive. So, having completed one more strawberry and shaded in a corner of pale green leaf, I gave up the struggle and set myself a different manual and mental exercise by starting to compose a letter of condolence to Angie.

However, the knowledge that it might not reach her until I was virtually out of contact and immured in some isolated cell of a rehearsal room soon made me break off yet again in mid-stream and ten minutes later I touched rock bottom in this long descent into procrastination by stretching out my hand for the telephone.

'I hope it doesn't matter calling you in working hours,' I said, 'but I haven't got your home number.'

'It's the same. I have an extension in the flat.'

'Oh well, in that case, perhaps you'd rather I left it till later?'

'Yes, that would be better. I have a bus-load of formidable American ladies with me at present, who know far more than I do about tapestry work, so I have to be on my toes.'

'Will you be in this evening?'

'Not sure, but lunch time would be all right.'

I was not displeased. It left me with only two hours to fritter away and gave me a chance to reflect on what I should say to her and what she might possibly say to me.

It did more than that, though, because – being one of those brief and usually deceptive periods when everything seemed to fall into place and wishing made it so – Robin turned out to be better than his word. Faced with the prospect of a long and difficult afternoon, he took an early lunch break and came home at half past twelve for a drink and a snack. Between mouthfuls he regaled me with a

141

report on the Dodie Watson post mortem.

'It looks like misadventure,' he began by saying. 'Leaving out all the technicalities, she died from a deficiency of insulin, first going into a coma, which, as you know, can be a normal hazard with that complaint.'

'But she'd been diabetic for years, ever since she was a child. She must have known better than anyone about such normal hazards and how to guard against them. Was there no suggestion at all of some other factor at work?'

'Not really. Small traces of pain killer, but nothing more sinister.'

'How small is small?'

'Two or three grains.'

'They weren't put up by a chemist in Dulwich, by any chance?'

'Not as far as I know. Why?'

'Just a thought. Any other developments?'

'No, and not likely to be now. There'll be an inquest, of course, but on present evidence I imagine the coroner will take the attitude that she got the pain killer mixed up with the insulin, or whatever it was she should have taken. It's logical, I suppose. X-ray photographs show her ankle to have been quite badly fractured, so she was probably in a certain amount of pain. Furthermore, she'd been through a bad period of shock and worry, not to mention lengthy interrogation, and had reason to be in a low and possibly confused state of mind. When you add chronic diabetes to that lot, it's hardly surprising that she wasn't at her most alert.'

'I expect you're right and you've certainly made out a good case for the defence, but I still can't help feeling that it's an odd coincidence that it should have happened just at this time.'

'Don't be dotty! Can't you see that it's because of the times that it did happen? It would have been far more remarkable if they'd been normal. Well, thanks for the meal. You have saved my life and I must now bustle off

142

and re-dedicate it to all those other sinister histories which are waiting on my desk.'

'Will you be very late back?'

'Fraid so, but I shan't want dinner, so don't wait up. And, with any luck, I'll be able to pack it in by midday tomorrow, so we might do something amusing at the weekend. It's your last one, let's not either of us forget.'

This lunch-time session had upset my timetable and it was nearly one thirty when I remembered about my call to Angie. As so often happens in these circumstances, before I could get to the telephone it had started to ring.

'You caught me at a bad moment,' she said in her laziest voice, 'and after I'd exchanged addresses with Louanne and Nancy and Marilyn and promised to visit with them next time I go to Cincinnati, I couldn't remember whether I was to call you back or the other way round.'

'Other way round, but I got held up too. I wanted to tell you how very sorry I was to hear about your sister,' I explained, feeling rather foolish now, since, by the sound of it, condolences were superfluous and her world was much the same place today as it had been yesterday.

'That was kind of you.'

'It must have been a hideous shock?'

'Yes, indeed. Poor Dodie! You never met her, did you?'

'No.'

'She didn't have much of a life after she grew up, poor girl. She was diabetic, you know. Also her marriage turned out badly and there were no children. Nothing ever seemed to work out right for her. Still, no good being maudlin about it now.'

'I was to have met her today, curiously enough.'

'Oh, really? Why was that?'

'At her wish, as a matter of fact. She'd hinted that she had something important she wanted to ask, or maybe tell me about. I suppose you have no idea what it could have been?'

143

It was one of the few occasions when I regretted not having a visual telephone because, after a perceptible pause, when she did speak Angie's voice had taken on a sharper note and it would have been interesting to see whether her expression matched it.

'None at all. You mean she got in touch and asked you to meet her?'

'No, it was arranged through my cousin, Ellen. We were both invited to lunch at her flat. You know Ellen Roxburgh, I expect? She's your sister Baba's god-daughter.'

'I know of her, but I hadn't realised that you and she were related.'

'Second cousins, to be precise. She is Toby Crichton's daughter. You met Toby at Beachclyffe.'

'Yes, yes, of course and at various other times over the years, but I never heard any mention of a daughter. Don't they get on or something?'

'Better than most, I would have said, but they are probably the kind of father and daughter who tend to talk to, rather than about, each other.'

For a conversation which had started out as an expression of condolence and sympathy, this one had deteriorated into something verging on acrimony, to which, if not wholly to blame, I had certainly contributed my share. Thinking that the time had come to introduce a conciliatory note, I said, 'Anyway, I didn't ring you up to talk about Ellen and Toby. I really wanted to know how you were getting through this sad time and whether there was any practical way I could help?'

'Very kind of you, but I don't think so, thanks all the same. What sort of practical help did you have in mind?'

'Well, for instance, I imagine the funeral will be in London?'

'I imagine it will too and probably on Wednesday, but nothing can be finalised until after the inquest. I gather

144

that's on Monday, but I don't have to go and we're leaving all the rest to Baba to cope with, as only she knows how.'

'That's rather what I was driving at. I know you don't always see eye to eye with her, so I thought it might save you the embarrassment of being there under her aegis, so to speak, if you were to spend Tuesday night here. We've converted the top floor into a sort of guest apartment, which Toby always uses when he comes to London, and Robin and I will both be out at work all day, so you could pretend it was an hotel.'

'And so much cheaper! How kind you are, Tessa! What have I done to deserve such treatment?'

'Taken me into your confidence, I suppose, trusted me with you innermost secrets. It always inspires gratitude, don't you think?'

Once again I could count the seconds before she said, 'Thanks, anyway. I'll be in touch with you as soon as we get our marching orders from Baba,' and rang off before I could say goodbye.

The afternoon ended, like its predecessor, with a telephone call to Ellen.

'I'm glad you've rung,' she said, 'because I wanted to ask you a favour. Can you and Robin come here for a drink about six thirty this evening?'

'Not Robin, he has to work late. I could come on my own, if that's any use.'

'Better still, in a way. You can probably deal with the situation more smoothly if he's not there to cramp your style.'

'Embarrass him by telling a lot of lies, you mean? What's up? Have you got a domestic crisis?'

'Only a mini-crisis, created by Peregrine.'

'What's he done? Challenged Jeremy to a duel?'

'No, that wouldn't be half so bad, Jeremy's a crack shot. The trouble is that, deprived of his dinner party tomorrow

145

night by yet another family fracas, Perry wishes to come here this evening to bid me farewell before departing to California. So it would be a great help if you could lend your support.'

'You think so? I doubt if Peregrine will see it in that light and I don't altogether fancy the idea of acting as your chaperon.'

'Don't be daft, that's not the idea at all. I can handle him quite well on my own, but I need a chaperon for Jeremy.'

'Oh, so he'll be there too, will he? Won't that make things rather awkward? Or are you too liberated to be bothered by such inhibitions?'

'On the contrary, they are just what do bother me. Perry doesn't know that Jeremy will be here, you see, and neither did I until just now because he usually plays bridge at his club on Friday evenings, if we haven't got anything special on. But his secretary rang up about half an hour ago to report that one of the four has dropped out and Jeremy will come straight here from the office.'

'All the makings of a jolly French farce!'

'Which is the last thing I need. So I thought, if you were here, you could ask Jeremy a few leading questions about trumping aces or how to invest your savings, which would leave Perry free to reel off his bit about undying love and how I'd ruined his life and so forth. With any luck, he'd then make a sad and dignified exit and Jeremy could trounce us both at Beggar My Neighbour, or maybe take us out to dinner somewhere.'

'Is he really so gone on you?'

'Who, Perry? Lord no, it's only a game. The truth is he doesn't want to marry this millionairess his mother has set her heart on. In fact, he's not keen to marry anyone. He has much more fun as an eligible bachelor and it suits him to pretend that his heart is broken and the woman he loves is married to another. At least, that's how I've always seen this hammy act he puts on, but, frankly, I'm beginning to wonder.'

146

'Wonder what?'

'Whether it goes deeper than that and I'm just being used as a double cover-up.'

'I suppose there must be worse things to be used as, but I can't think of one at the moment. What gave you such a horrid idea?'

'You remember when Jeremy and I went to Paris the week before last? While we were driving through the tunnel at Heathrow there was another car ahead of us and by the time we came out at the other end we were right close up behind it. It was a bashed-up sort of Mini thing with a girl driving it and I could have sworn the man with her was Perry. I never found out, though, because we were going to Terminal One and they zoomed off towards one of the others.'

'Very mysterious! Still, one swallow doesn't make a summer.'

'No, but someone else told me they'd run into him in Dublin, of all places, only a few weeks before that. It was at the Curragh, or one of those, and he always told me he hated race meetings. Makes you think, doesn't it?'

'Sure does, but devious or not, he sounds a lot more lively than that dreary Steven. In fact, I'm quite keen to meet him. See you in about an hour.'

FIFTEEN

I was not disappointed and nor was it hard to see why even the perceptive Ellen had failed to gauge which way this particular cat would jump. Whatever his motive, the evening rapidly moved on to a level far outside the guidelines laid down for it by Mrs J. Roxburgh.

I was not much impressed by the rest of her assessment either. It was true that he looked like a sleeker, more affluent version of his brother and was wearing a handmade shirt and shoes, but the bowler hat and old school tie were not in evidence. Perhaps he kept those for California, or perhaps the rather more free and easy manners which obtain there had done something to tone down the complacency and conceit which life with his mother had bred in him. His most notable feature, however, was his eyes, which had a pale and luminous quality about them and seemed to change from blue to green with the light. They made him look untrustworthy, but not unattractive.

Admittedly, my favourable opinion may have been due in part to the fact that from the moment of introduction he went out of his way to be flattering and attentive and one cannot ask much more of a handsome and successful young man. Furthermore, while constantly reminding myself that I possessed the inestimable virtue of being married and therefore, with any luck, unattainable, it was clear from the knowledgeable way he talked about plays and films I had appeared in that he had either enjoyed them as much as he claimed, or else had gone to some pains to mug up about them in advance. In my view, one was as good as the other.

148

Some young women might have resented having their pale and loitering knight snatched from under their noses by an interloping second cousin, but not Ellen. Her idea of unmitigated bliss was to be presented with the unexpected chance to spend an evening alone with Jeremy and, when she saw the way things were going, she registered amazement and amusement in quick succession, followed almost as rapidly by open encouragement. It ended with Peregrine taking me out to dinner.

'I've been dying for this moment, I must tell you,' he said when, after much pomp and finger-snapping, the head waiter had conducted us to our table in the manner of the Lord Chamberlain personally escorting a pair of racegoers to their box at Ascot.

'Oh, good!'

'And that's wonderful too.'

'What is?' I asked, trying to stop my eyes straying to the menu.

'Not throwing in a lot of false modesty about now that it's come, you hope I'm not disappointed and so on. Just "oh, good!" in a polite voice, as though I had told you it had stopped raining. I love people with that kind of assurance.'

'Is that what you love about Ellen?'

'Oh yes, among a lot of other unique and marvellous qualities. That's why I've never forgiven my mother for keeping us apart for all those years. But for that, I often think, how different my life might have been. Ellen has the power to make me feel better than I am.'

'Yes, she does have that effect on people. It was quite a shrewd observation.'

'Thank you. Aren't you curious to know why I've been dying to meet you?'

'Yes, naturally.'

'It is because, so far as I know, you're the only woman

149

alive who puts the fear of God into my mama.'

At this point the waiter arrived to take our order and, as it was something which could not be done in a hurry, five or six minutes went by before the conversation could be resumed.

'Your mother seems to figure rather prominently in your life,' I suggested.

'Oh, I hope not. I do try not to let her. It has become the major task of my life.'

'Then I am afraid you still have some way to go. I haven't known you for more than an hour and you've already referred to her in that special voice no fewer than five times.'

'Really? Can you be sure of that?'

'Certainly. Three times when you were talking to Ellen, twice within the last ten minutes.'

'How terrifyingly observant you are! I believe my mother is right to be so afraid of you.'

'That is the sixth time,' I reminded him, 'and you still haven't told me why she is.'

'As it happens, I was going to ask you. I suppose the answer is coming ahead of the question, but it has been puzzling me. It's so unlike her, you know. Normally, she blasts and blunders her way through life, caring not a jot for any man's opinion, far less any woman's.'

'So to what do I owe this unique distinction, do you suppose?'

'All I can tell you is that I was present on a recent occasion when she was trying to pump Clarrie about you. Clarissa Jones, the actress. I gather she's a friend of yours?'

'So she is, but I had the impression that she was also persona non grata with your mater?'

'Not any more. In fact, she is almost alone among attractive young women in posing no threat. Having made a great play for my brother and been cast aside like a worn-out glove . . .'

150

'That's one way of putting it.'

'I can only repeat what I've been told, but whichever side did the casting, the glove is likely to remain where it is and Clarrie, who, even with all her previous faults, always had social and entertainment value, has now become a favourite at court. Which, as I've mentioned already, is more than can be said for you.'

'What tales has Clarrie been spinning about me? They are bound to be a pack of lies, but it would be interesting to know what they consisted of.'

'Then I shall tell you, but you mustn't be too cross with her. I feel sure she only tells the sort of lies that people want to hear, which shows a decent desire to please. In your case, the line was that once upon a time you were just a sweet, good-natured simpleton, struggling like her to make good in the theatre.'

'That's two whoppers, for a start. I was never sweet or simple and Clarrie has never had to struggle for anything in her life. What's supposed to have changed me?'

'She blames it on your husband. It would appear that ever since your marriage, you have become more dedicated to his career and advancement than your own.'

'She must be slipping. The idea that I could do anything to advance his career is too ludicrous to be taken seriously by anyone. Besides, what would be so terrible about it if I could? Surely she can do better than that?'

'Oh, it doesn't end there. She claims that, as a result of your tireless efforts on his behalf, you have developed a flair for criminology, all your own. She also maintains, quoting chapter and verse, that there have been numerous cases which you have played an unofficial part in solving. According to Clarrie, this has never been made public, but there are hordes of people in the theatre who would confirm every word. All quite unfounded, presumably?'

'No, not altogether, I have to admit. But she was blowing up one small incident into something much more

151

sensational than it actually was. The fact is that Clarrie and I were in a play together the year before last and someone in the cast was murdered. It had to be an inside job, a member of the company, that is, and, since I had been living and working with them for weeks, I naturally knew far more about their private feuds and jealousies than an outsider could have discovered in a couple of years.'

'Although I suppose that would have applied equally to the rest of them? The difference, according to Clarrie, being that you were the only one to use that special knowledge to catch out the murderer.'

'Which isn't quite fair either. The real difference was that I'd known one of the cast since I was a small child and that's what really gave me the edge. And, in any case, none of it had anything to do with furthering Robin's career. It wouldn't have affected him, one way or the other, if it had remained unsolved for all eternity. That's the truth and you are at liberty to pass it on to your mother, if you think she'd be interested.'

'Oh, she will, although whether it will allay her fears about you is another question.'

'Why, though? Has she committed some crime and is afraid of my finding out?'

'Oh, undoubtedly. That would have to be at the bottom of it, wouldn't you say?'

'I have no idea, but you seem to take it very coolly.'

'I have learnt to live with it, my darling. There is a strong criminal streak in my family, you know.'

'I didn't know.'

'Amazing how they've always got away with it, really. A mixture of shameless bluff and the indestructible belief that they possess some divine right which sets them apart from ordinary mortals. Someone at Eton once told me that my grandfather was celebrated for cheating at cards, but he always got away with it simply by looking stern and noble. No one had the nerve to complain.'

152

'I suppose that's not exactly criminal, just rather absurd?'

'It is verging on the very slightly criminal, if you happen to be playing for high stakes, wouldn't you say? And that was only the tip of the iceberg. It is always said that one of the Irish cousins damn nearly got sent down for setting fire to his own property, in order to claim the insurance. But of course the real heinous crimes never came to light. Did you know, for instance, that one of my aunts murdered her husband?'

'Yes, I had heard that one,' I replied dismissively, the better to provoke him into further indiscretions. The conversation had taken an interesting turn and it seemed to me that the longer I could keep up the pretence of bland indifference the deeper he would dig into the pile of family skeletons in an attempt to shake me out of it. In doing so, I experienced a passing pang of regret for having to divert so much of my attention away from the dinner that was being set before us, since it really deserved silent and serious appreciation.

Peregrine may also have become conscious of this, or else of the need to restrain himself, for he made no comment, but spent the next two or three minutes enquiring whether the dish was up to scratch, comparing it with one he had eaten in New York the previous week and in signalling to the waiter to charge our glasses.

It was all done in a somewhat distrait and perfunctory manner, however, and very soon, evidently unable to hold out any longer, he asked, 'Who told you about my murderous aunt?'

'Gossip, rumour, hearsay. The sort of tittle-tattle that always gets around when some man who has become a liability to his wife conveniently dies in his sleep.'

'You really do know, don't you?' Peregrine muttered, looking rather shaken. 'It wasn't just bluff. My mother would have a fit if she could hear you.'

153

'Then I must be careful not to repeat it in her presence. Although I don't see why she should be so terrified of that particular story getting around. It's not as though she had any part in it. Or had she?'

'It's a relief to find there's something you don't know, Tessa. No, as far as I know, she hadn't, but your knowing about it would confirm her worst fears. What other scandals in my family are filed away in your dossier?'

'Oh, any amount. I'm also acquainted with members of the other branch, you see. Collaterals would be the word, I suppose.'

'Laura, you mean?'

'Yes, Laura and. . .' I had been about to add 'and her brother Tom' but thought better of it and substituted, 'And her daughter and son-in-law. He's a policeman too, you know, in the same branch as Robin.'

'Although I doubt if they're so eager to tell you about their own little falls from grace?'

'How can I say? If I knew which you were thinking of, I should be able to tell you whether I'd heard about them or not.'

'Oh yes, very sharp and I'm sure if my mother were here, she'd fall for it and launch forth on the instant. Probably be trapped into seeing it as quite a fair bargain until after she got home and thought about it.'

'But not you, of course?'

'No, but I'll offer you a different one. If I let you into a secret about those Lampeters which I'm pretty sure will come as news to you, will you promise me one thing?'

'That's no better than mine. How can I promise something until I know what it is?'

'To put it bluntly, I'd like you to stop hounding my mother.'

'Me personally?'

'Naturally. I wouldn't expect you to promise such a thing on behalf of someone else and, in any case, there

154

would be no need for it. She has created a number of follies in her time, mostly out of vanity or the desire to impress and appear all-powerful, but to the best of my belief she has not been guilty of any serious crime. In short, my dearest Tessa, if I may so address you, what she fears is not prosecution but social ostracism and, for some reason, she has convinced herself that your interest or curiosity in her private activities is liable to bring that about. Having met you, I am prepared to say that this time she has displayed somewhat more acumen than she usually does.'

'And so, if I give you my word that I, personally, have no interest in her private life and that it is not and never has been my object to humiliate her in the eyes of the world, everything will be all right?'

'Everything will be just fine.'

'Then I do give it.'

'That's very handsome of you!'

'No, it's not. It cost me no sacrifice at all and may I remind you that your side of the bargain is still outstanding?'

'I think it will amuse you. At any rate, you will be forced to admit that not all those poor, persecuted, misunderstood Lampeters are quite as saintly as they would have us believe. For instance, did you know that the brother, Tom, who now, according to rumour, goes around with shaven head converting the heathen, had once done a spell in jug?'

'No, I didn't. What was it for?'

'Forging cheques. He got away with quite a packet too, some of it my mother's, until he was run in.'

'And I suppose it was she who told you this?'

'Wrong, as it happens. It was my aunt Dodie who told me.'

'The one who died the other day?'

'And on whose account I was sent for in a great hurry all the way from California. For a woman who, up to then, had created no breath of sensation whatever, she certainly made up for it during her last few weeks on earth.'

'When did she tell you?'

'Years ago, when I was a mere lad. She had no business to, of course, but any audience, even one of such tender years, was meat and drink to her. She may not have created any sensations of her own, but other people's were what she lived by and being first to break the news became her mission in life.'

'Well, thank you for telling me,' I said. 'It is always fascinating to hear of the threads which are woven into a family background, but since it happened such a long time ago and he has served his sentence, I don't consider it so very important. After all, I believe you got the best of our bargain.'

I was pleased to see Peregrine look somewhat complacent on hearing this, for in fact it was the only major deviation from the truth which I had made throughout the evening and it was satisfactory to know that I had got away with it.

Robin had arrived home an hour ahead of me and was looking aggrieved about it, so I listened for a full five minutes while he worked off his ill humour in describing the disappointments, heartbreaks and frustrations with which his path had been strewn since our last encounter. At the end of it, quite cheered up again, he said, 'Oh well, it will sort itself out, I daresay. What sort of an evening did you have?'

'Not bad,' I replied, 'compared to yours,' and told him a little about my dinner with Peregrine, touching on the many dainty dishes that had been set before us and adding, 'Only that had its element of heartbreak and frustration too.'

'Why was that? Did he expect you to pay your share?'

'Oh, dear me, no, he's very polished and he treats

women as though they were cherished half-wits. That's the American influence, I expect. I am told they can be very chauvinist in that way.'

'It probably comes to the same thing in the end, whichever way you treat them. What was so agonising about the dinner?'

'Not being able to do justice to it. I had to pay too much attention to what he was saying.'

'And what was that, apart from polished remarks about what a beautiful, angelic half-wit you were?'

'Something quite revealing, I think. He didn't realise it, of course, but if what he told me was true, he may have provided me with the last peg on which to hang a theory I've worked out about how and why the house at Mallings was burnt down and who was responsible. Would you like me to try it out on you, or are you too tired?'

'No, but you're too late, I'm afraid. The experts, you will be astonished to hear, have also been giving the matter their attention and they have already discovered why it happened and who was responsible.'

'Oh no, you can't mean it! Why didn't you tell me?'

'I was going to, as soon as I got home this evening, but you weren't here and it went right out of my head. What a shame! You might have been able to concentrate on that lovely dinner after all.'

'Okay, don't rub it in. Why did it happen and who was responsible?'

'Evidently, it was caused by a short circuit and the culprit was most likely a rat who had gnawed through the electric wires.'

It was not until he had finished speaking that I realised I had been holding my breath and I let it out gradually, for fear of his sensing my relief.

'And what about the woman who died?' I asked when I had completed this exercise. 'Any theories about her?'

'The popular one is that she was some vagrant, who

157

knew the house was rarely occupied and was using it as an occasional base.'

'And Dodie had no suggestions to make about the woman who had been impersonating her?'

'It seems not. She was questioned on several occasions and they hadn't finished with her when she died. On the whole, she was not a satisfactory witness. Contradicted herself endlessly and got badly tangled up. The conclusion was that, although she never admitted it, she hadn't been impersonated at all, but for some reason, which has now died with her, she rented the place herself, but didn't want anyone to know. So it's all been a waste of time and she might just as well have stayed in Denmark.'

There were various comments I could have made about this, but I could tell that he was still a shade put out by the experience of returning home late at night to an empty house after the long day's slog and I considered it wiser to keep them to myself.

So we talked for a while of other matters and, as we were toiling upstairs to bed, he said, 'Oh, by the way, there was a telephone message for you. Did you see it?'

'No, I forgot to look. Who was it from?'

'According to Mrs Cheeseman, her name was Papworth and she rang to say she would be spending Tuesday night with us and will call you tomorrow to arrange the details. At least, that was the gist of it and I must say I do think you might let me know when you invite strange women to stay. One of these days, I suppose I shall stagger home at midnight to find one of them sitting in an armchair and drinking my whisky.'

'I couldn't let you know because you weren't here and anyway she's not a strange woman in that sense. To everyone except Mrs Cheeseman her name is Petworth and she is your sergeant's mother-in-law's half-sister.'

Robin had Saturday off, for once, so we were able to give

ourselves up to a whole day of pleasure and self-indulgence, which, taken in moderation, I have always found to be the soundest cure for frayed nerves and sour tempers. The fact that it was also my last weekend before the axe of regular employment fell on me gave an added zest to the occasion and no doubt did most to restore Robin's good humour, as I daresay he could hardly wait for a return to the pattern of irregular hours he was accustomed to.

To my everlasting gratitude, he takes my career almost as seriously as I do and would no more have thought of complaining if it kept me out till all hours than I would have contemplated telephoning Scotland Yard to demand that the case be dropped at once, as his dinner was getting spoilt.

By Sunday evening the mood had become so mellow that I considered it safe to re-open the subject of Angie's impending visit and to explain why she needed a refuge on Tuesday night.

'Did she call you again?' he asked.

'Just now, when you were putting the car to bed. I asked her what time she'd be arriving and she said about six, if that would be okay.'

'And would it?'

'You know it wouldn't. I explained that there would be no one here to let her in after four o'clock because I probably wouldn't be back before six thirty or seven and you certainly wouldn't.'

'So what did you arrange?'

'She'll come earlier, some time during the afternoon before Mrs Cheeseman leaves, dump her suitcase, collect a set of keys and come back at six, or whenever it suits her. So then I asked her if she'd be here for dinner and she said yes, if it wouldn't be a bore and a nuisance.'

'And what did you say to that?'

'The usual things, though privately thinking that it

159

might be a great bore for you having her here, unadulterated, so to speak, for a whole evening.'

'I see no way to avoid it, though. It is hardly a suitable occasion for a party. Besides, you're bound to be worn to a rag and in need of an early night when you do get back.'

'Which is why I thought I might ring Toby in the morning and invite him to join us. It would be a sort of compromise.'

'Not a very brilliant one, though. It would be an improvement, I agree, but I hardly think he'll want to come unless he can spend the night and he can't do that if someone else is occupying his room.'

'No, that's all taken care of, he can stay with Ellen. They're dining out on Tuesday, won't be home until after he's in bed and Jeremy will have bustled off to the City long before he gets up. With any luck, they won't have to meet at all and he can spend a peaceful morning with Ellen.'

'Well, you certainly seem to be going to a great deal of trouble for your friend Mrs Petworth,' Robin said, 'and you've certainly got everything cut and dried. Any outsider could be forgiven for suspecting that there might be something more to it than just a simple act of kindness.'

'But you know better?'

'Me? No, I just hope to be forgiven too.'

SIXTEEN

By some miracle, it was only ten minutes to six when the taxi dropped me at Beacon Square on Tuesday evening, but that was to be the last cause for rejoicing to come my way for several hours.

Things started to fall apart as soon as I reached the front door because it was off the latch and needed only a push to swing it open. One or two explanations for this phenomenon flitted into my mind, including the unlikely one that Mrs Cheeseman had forgotten to lock it behind her when she left. However, there was to be some delay in getting to the root of the matter because a set of keys lay on the hall table beside the message pad which had several items written on it, the first of which being the request from my agent to call her back the minute I came in. Below this Mrs Cheeseman had inscribed one of her more lucid efforts, which read as follows:

'Mrs Petworth phoned to say she'd been held up, coming later, but not to expect her before seven.'

The mystery of the front door having now been relegated to second place on the agenda, I was about to dial my agent's number when it occurred to me that it would be a sensible idea to collect a gin and tonic, with which to fortify myself against whatever verbal onslaught might be in store.

So I trotted off to the kitchen to fill up the ice bowl, which I then carried, with half a lemon balanced on its lid, a few steps inside the drawing room. This door was also slightly open and, having no free hand, I gave it a sharp

161

kick and was instantly confronted by a scene of desolation and havoc.

In the moment or two of paralysed shock which ensued I remember thinking that modern burglars were really getting above themselves to have reached the point of breaking and entering the premises of detective inspectors from Scotland Yard. Then natural reflexes took over again and I advanced a few more steps into the room. It was then that, so far as I could tell, part of the ceiling collapsed on top of me and still, for some insane reason, clinging to the ice bucket, I fell forward and passed out.

When I came to I was lying face down across the threshold, as I could tell from the position of various chair and table legs within the narrow line of vision. I did not attempt to move, though, because my head was aching and I was afraid that I had broken several bones in my arms, which were not only giving off a fiery pain, but seemed to be twisted in a most unnatural way behind my back. However, since my head appeared to be still attached to the rest of me, I turned it cautiously sideways, to test whether my neck was also intact.

This was a mistake, for it was as though the movement had touched off a nerve, causing the pain to spread down through my legs and ankles. I was becoming badly frightened by this time and, in an effort to hold on to sanity and not start whimpering, I remained perfectly still, drawing in deep and regular breaths and trying to pretend that I was lying in bed and practising my own brand of relaxation and sleep-inducing therapy.

It worked, up to a point, because in the comparative calm which it brought I gradually became aware of extraneous sounds and movements, indicating that I was not alone. Someone close behind me was also doing some heavy breathing, louder and more laboured than my own, and a sharp spasm of pain in one ankle was accompanied by an audible grunt. It dawned on me at last that the aches

162

and pains were not due to injuries inflicted by the thunderbolt, but to the cords with which I was now being trussed and bound.

This operation had evidently been completed, though, because the next sensation was of a hand on my shoulder and I found myself being pushed far enough sideways to be able to look a few feet upwards from ground level. It was not a sight to gladden the heart, however, because what it showed me was the upper half of a man on his knees, looking down on me. He was wearing grey woollen gloves and had a grey hood over his head, with slits cut into it, so that all I could see of his face were his eyes. They happened to be the last thing I wanted to look at, so I closed my own and allowed myself to fall forward again, face down on the carpet and waiting for worse to befall.

What in fact befell was the ringing of the front door bell, followed by a minute or so of total silence, in which I and, presumably, my assailant stopped breathing altogether. Then it rang again and I heard a muted kind of sob and some scuffling noises. There followed another period of silence, broken this time by noises off, including a high-pitched human voice, cut off by the slam of a door. Then the same voice, sounding clearer now, called out from the hall:

'Is anyone there?'

'In here,' I croaked and in two minutes Angie was beside me, tugging at the cords and asking me repeatedly whether I was all right, which struck me as a fatuous question in the circumstances and not worth the trouble of answering. However, she improved on this performance, once I was released and able to sit up, by rubbing my wrists and ankles to get the circulation moving and by suggesting that a stiff brandy might help this process along.

'Did you see him?' I asked while she was pouring it out.

163

'Not clearly, I'm sorry to say. The door opened and whoever it was came flying out and pushed me off balance. By the time I'd pulled myself together he was down on the pavement, dodging between two cars which were parked on the kerb. I was so rattled that I didn't think of running after him. I don't suppose it would have done any good if I had.'

'Was he still wearing the hood?'

'No hood, no. I seem to remember he had some kind of scarf round his neck.'

'But you didn't see his face?'

'Only a sort of sideways glimpse. It all happened in a couple of seconds and, as I told you, my reflexes weren't at their sharpest. Here, drink this down and tell me what I should do next.'

'Well, obviously, what we need now is a policeman. Would you mind dealing with it for me? The number, in case you don't know it, is. . .no, hang on a minute, you'll need his extension as well. It's all written down under R for Robin in the green book on the table beside the telephone and there's a chair there as well, in case it takes you a few minutes to get through to him.'

Evidently, it needed more than a few, for she was away for what seemed like at least ten. However, I didn't interfere, since she was obviously quite capable in her own languid way and I was feeling too weak and shattered to want to take over the job myself. I remained in a recumbent position, massaging my legs occasionally and jerking my shoulders about, while looking round the room to see whether I could spot anything missing.

Apparently, though, he had been one of the professional and selective type of thieves because, although cushions had been tossed around, tables and chairs overturned and the contents of one or two drawers scattered over the floor, I could not call to mind anything that should have been there and was not. One or two pictures had been knocked askew, but there were no lighter coloured spaces on the walls and the rugs and some semi-valuable pieces of bronze and china had not been disturbed.

Angie came back at this point in my survey and I asked her how she had got on.

'All in hand. He's on his way round.'

'How did he take it?'

'Calmly. He was worried about you, though.'

'I trust you told him there was no need to be?'

'Naturally, and the next question was whether any other rooms had been ransacked, or only this one.'

'Oh God, yes, I ought to have thought of that. I'd better have a look before he gets here. Will you come with me? I know the kitchen's all right, but he may have tried the dining room.'

'I should call it unlikely.'

'Why? There's quite a lot of silver stashed away in there.'

'And so, if it was silver he was after, that's the first room he'd have looked in. And, having swiped it, would have made off. He wouldn't then have moved on to try his luck in here.'

'You were quite right,' I told her, shutting the last of the sideboard drawers. 'That's a relief, but I suppose we'd better just make sure about the bedrooms.'

'May as well take this with me, while I'm at it,' Angie said, gathering up her suitcase, in another demonstration of her practical approach to a crisis.

It was the same story on the first floor, where all was as neat as it only ever was for the first two or three hours after Mrs Cheeseman's departure.

'And here's your room,' I said, opening a door on the landing above. 'There's a tiny sitting room opposite and the bathroom's next door.'

It might have been the pristine condition of the other beds which drew my attention to the fact that the cover on

165

this one was pulled slightly sideways. Straightening it as I spoke, I went on, 'If you feel like having a bath now, go ahead. Mrs Cheeseman seems to keep the hot tap running permanently until she leaves at four, but the water should have heated up again by now.'

Once again proving that she had a firmer grasp of the situation than I had, Angie said, 'Very tempting, after traipsing round London all day, but I imagine your husband will want to ask me about my encounter with the intruder, so I'd better be available when he gets back. I'll just wash and hang up a couple of things and then join you downstairs.'

I was halfway down myself when I heard a key turn in the front door lock, causing a moment or two of frantic alarm, since I could not believe that enough time had passed for Robin to have arrived already. However, it was only Toby.

'I know I'm early,' he explained, evidently mistaking my ghastly pallor and trembling hands for displeasure, 'but for some reason, Mrs Parkes seemed in rather a hurry to get rid of me.'

'Gala Night at the Bingo Hall, perhaps?'

'Maybe. She kept telling me that I ought to make an early start to avoid the evening rush hour. She knows as well as I do that at six o'clock the traffic is all rushing the other way, but I pride myself on being able to take a hint, so here I am.'

'And most welcome. I'm only sorry you didn't indulge her a little further and leave at four. You might have seen off our burglar.'

'Oh, so that's why you're looking so put out. What did he take?'

'Nothing, as far as I can see. Perhaps he arrived only just ahead of me and hadn't had time to get down to business. Anyway, Angie appeared in the nick of time and saved me from dire discomfort, if not worse, and he decided the

166

place was getting altogether too crowded and hurtled off. It's a long and highly dramatic story, but if you don't mind I'll save it till Robin gets here, because I haven't the strength to go through it twice. Give yourself a drink and make one for me. I'm on brandy this evening.'

'So you don't mean to report it?' I asked Robin half an hour later.

'There wouldn't be much point, would there? It's not the kind of advice I'd hand out to the customers, and I suppose a reluctance to set myself up as the joke of the century has something to do with it, but I can't see how reporting it would serve any practical purpose. In the first place, neither of us can find anything missing. You had a bad experience, but there are no scars to show for it, apart from a certain dottiness from time to time. Furthermore, since you say he was wearing gloves there won't be any prints and, finally, we can't give so much as a rough description of what he looked like, because all you saw of him were his eyes.'

'Yes, just his eyes,' I agreed solemnly.

'And you didn't do much better, did you, Angie? I suppose I may call you Angie, since this has hardly been what you might call a formal introduction?'

'Oh, please do, and I'm sorry to be such a wash-out. I got the impression of fair hair, clean-shaven and slightly under average height. Five foot eight or nine, perhaps.'

'So there's the picture. A man who looked pretty much like half a million others in London, quick on his feet and possessing a pair of eyes.'

'Yes, a pair of eyes,' I repeated in a sing-song voice.

Robin frowned. 'Are you really feeling all right, Tessa?'

'Oh yes, fine, thank you. This brandy is doing wonders for me.'

'Perhaps it is hardly my place to say so,' Toby remarked, 'but I should have thought the only question

167

worth asking was how this marauder got in? Not a word has been said about forced locks or broken windows, I notice.'

'For the simple reason,' Robin announced, 'that there are none. There appears to be something seriously wrong with our security arrangements and, to be honest, I prefer to make my own private investigations first. I suppose it will mean a little chat with Mrs Cheeseman in the morning.'

'I sincerely hope not,' I told him. 'You have your valid reasons for wishing to hush this up and I have mine too, Mrs Cheeseman being the principal one. Any questions of that kind would instantly be taken as a direct accusation and she would give notice on the spot. If you imagine I could run this house, do all the cooking and cleaning, answer the telephone and minister to your needs when, for the next two months, I shall be leaving the house at dawn every morning and not getting back till dusk, there must also be something seriously wrong with our lines of communication. You will oblige me by not referring to the subject in her presence.

'Besides,' I added on a calmer note during the hush which greeted this outburst, 'I doubt if it will be necessary. I daresay we shall have found out all we need to know before the evening is over. And now, if you'll excuse me, I'll go and get on with the dinner.'

Robin started all over again about taking it easy and letting someone else do the work, or, better still, going out to some quiet little nearby restaurant, but I scarcely listened. All the while he was talking I had my eye on Angie and I could see that, unlike him, she had no illusions that I was suffering from delayed shock or mild concussion. She had understood exactly what I was on about.

SEVENTEEN

On principle, Robin and I prefer not to discuss important matters while eating, so during dinner I prattled on about my first day at work, throwing in a few imitations of our director and other members of the company. Toby weighed in with some horrendous tales of behind-the-scenes life at Roakes Common, all of which he claimed had been reported to him by Mrs Parkes. Robin, not attempting to match these performances, obligingly kept up a steady interjection of exclamations of amusement or disgust, as the case might call for, and Angie sat through it all with an air of total composure.

When it was nearly over and we were discussing whether to stay where we were or move back to the other room for coffee, she stood up and announced her intention, rather than asked permission, of making a telephone call. There was an extension in this, as in almost every other room in the house, but I suggested that she might prefer to use the one in the hall.

'Aren't you afraid she will walk straight out of the house?' Toby asked when she had closed the door behind her.

'No, she is too intelligent for that.'

'I sense a lack of continuity about this evening,' Robin complained. 'It is like watching a film in which every third reel has been cut out by the censor. I am unable to find any particular reason why she should walk out of the house and nor do I understand why she couldn't have made her telephone call either before dinner or after we had finished.'

169

'Presumably she wanted to reduce the chances of being overheard,' I explained, 'but perhaps even more important was the question of timing. I expect she had worked out how long it would take to get to Victoria Station, plus the train journey and bus ride the other end, and had decided that nine o'clock was about the earliest moment to ring up.'

'Thank you very much. There goes reel number five.'

'Well, just contain yourself for a little longer. Angie is sure to tell us all about it when she comes back. Including the last reel of all, which, I have to confess, I edited out myself. Even you weren't shown that one, Toby, which was a pretty shabby reward for that long, hot afternoon you spent trailing round the Sussex coast.'

Angie did not appear to be in any hurry to enlighten us when she returned, however, so I attempted to help things along by giving her a prod:

'Did you get through all right?'

'No, I'll have to try again later. There was no reply.'

'How strange!'

'It has been known.'

'Oh, indeed, all the time, but you were out there for nearly ten minutes and it usually dawns after one or two, if there's no one there.'

'I thought there might be a fault on the line, so I got the operator to try it for me.'

'Oh, I see! So you found it rather strange too?'

'Really, Tessa,' Robin protested, 'we all know you've had a nasty shock, but is it necessary to behave quite so rudely?'

'Maybe not, but, as you say, I've had a shock. I've been trussed up like an oven-ready chicken and, for all I know, that man intended to wring my neck, so naturally I'm a little on edge. Never mind, I'll leave you now and make the coffee and you can all relax.'

* * *

170

'I remember your telling me, Angie, that you practically lived on it, so I've made a double quantity,' I said when I poured it out. 'Did he really mean to kill me, or didn't he tell you?'

Robin replaced his cup in the saucer in a careful and deliberate way, but this time it was Toby who jumped in with the protest:

'My impression is that it's no longer the reels that are mixed up. Someone has now put an entirely new film in the projector. You agree, Robin?'

'Absolutely. How could either of you guess what his intentions were, or anything at all about him? You say he never spoke a word and you couldn't see his face, only his eyes.'

'Only his eyes.'

'As you keep repeating, only his eyes. And Angie had even less to go on. All she got was a fleeting back view from some distance away.'

'Yes, but she didn't need more than that, not even as much. She had recognised him as soon as she came inside the house and shut the front door. Isn't that right, Angie?'

'You know, I think it might not be a bad plan to get the doctor round, just to give you a look-over,' Robin said, answering for her. 'A sedative might be the thing at this stage.'

'No, don't worry, I'm quite all right and, if Angie doesn't feel like explaining, I'll do it for her and she can tell me if I go wrong.'

'What a good idea!' she agreed. 'It is bound to be much more interesting, coming from you.'

'So, leaving aside those eyes for the moment, the reason why you recognised him as soon as you came into the hall, if not before, was that you saw a bunch of keys lying beside the message pad on the table. No doubt they looked suspiciously like the Yale and mortice keys of a front door and I would hazard a guess that the sight of them set off, or

171

perhaps merely reinforced the first wave of apprehension. So, naturally, you walk over to take a closer look and in doing so you see the message from Mrs Cheeseman, telling me that you had been unable to call and collect them. That was when you knew for certain who it was who had bolted out of the house and pushed you aside when you rang the bell. How am I doing?'

'Do go on!' Angie said, helping herself to more coffee.

'No, hang on a minute,' Robin said, 'because I really must try and get this sorted out before either of you says another word. Either Angie is humouring you because, like me, she feels you are not quite yourself just now, or else she understands what you are driving at, which I most certainly do not. How could a note from Mrs Cheeseman tell anyone anything about the identity of an intruder who turned up after she had gone home?'

'Well, of course, it wasn't from her at all, that's the whole point. I remember thinking it was a remarkably coherent message for her, but my mind at that point was dwelling mainly on things like kicking off my shoes and downing a strong drink and, in any case, the true explanation was far too melodramatic to have occurred to me. All the same, I ought to have been a bit more alert because she had got Angie's name right and spelt it right, which is practically unheard of, only of course the forger couldn't have known that.'

I sensed that Robin was about to lodge another protest, but thought better of it and also that Toby was paying above average attention to what was going on, but most of my own was reserved for Angie. To all appearances, she remained quite unruffled, making no attempt either to admit or deny that she understood what I was talking about.

'Of course, it could not be proved, in the legal sense, that it was a forgery and the work of your brother Tom,' I told her, 'but the fact that it had vanished and there was a

172

blank page in its place when I walked past it to let Toby in is proof enough for me. It can only have been you who removed and destroyed the one with all the messages which was there when I came home, and what other reason can you have had than that, having re-read it and drawn your own conclusions while making your telephone call to Robin, you had decided to cover his tracks for him?'

'Please go on!' Angie said again.

'I must. Having stuck my neck out this far, I can't just leave it dangling, although part of the next bit will have to be guesswork, based on what I might have done myself in those circumstances and what I know of you, personally.'

'What do you know of me, personally?'

'That you're resourceful and intelligent,' I replied, ticking off the items on my fingers. 'You have your emotions tightly locked in, have cultivated an air of detachment the better to conceal them and, according to first hand information, can be ruthless and capable of taking enormous risks. Most important of all, you have an obsessive, most likely well-founded dislike of your sister Baba. I think Laura probably runs you a close second there and I also believe it to be the reason why you both grew up with this special feeling of protectiveness and affection for Tom. Naturally, you would have championed anyone who was Baba's enemy and, as the only boy in the family and the one to whom your father left his money, she would obviously have been more passionately resentful and jealous of him than either of his sisters. There was still more to it than that, though. You took after your mother, in many ways, and it is second nature to you to support the underdog. That may be why you always remained such good friends with Laura, but Tom was the real protégé and you were always on hand to smooth the path for him and stand between him and harsh reality. He learnt at a very early age that he could take all that was going and, if there was a price to be paid, you would somehow

173

stump up.'

'In a superficial way, that's not a bad assessment,' Angie said, pouring her third cup of coffee. 'I realised from the start that you were a force to be reckoned with and I warned the other two. Doesn't anyone else want more coffee? There is plenty here.'

'Not for me, thank you,' Toby said. 'It keeps me awake and I think I am collecting enough insomnia fodder for one night.'

'Robin?'

'Yes, I will have some, please. I gather from your comment that what Tessa told us was on the mark?'

'Why not? It has done nothing, so far as I can see, to connect Tom with tonight's episode. As you say, Tessa, that note from your daily help, whether written by herself or not, seems to have disappeared, but what of it? Or was it just those eyes you saw between the slits in his hood that gave you the idea he was Tom?'

'Well, something of the sort struck me at the time, but I was too shocked and scared to take it in properly. I imagine the most benign pair of eyes would look strange and menacing if you saw them glaring at you from behind an old sock, but there was an extra quality about these, a sort of fanatical glint, which I'd seen somewhere before. It was only later that I remembered where it was. Of course, if he'd been wearing his beard this evening, it might have made all the difference.'

Robin started to explode again. 'For God's sake, Tessa, you're going off the rails. How could he not have been wearing it if he had one? It is not a thing you can take on and off, as circumstances dictate.'

'Oh yes it is, specially if you happen to have any experience in the theatre. He did have one, but it had to come off before he could show himself in Mallings, for the simple reason that the first and sometimes the only thing people notice about a man with a beard is his beard. Then,

174

of course, when Toby and I were sighted in Beachclyffe he needed to grow it again. So he brought out the false one which was kept for such emergencies and he and Angie stuck it on. It was tricky, though, because, being a pro myself, I was likely to be harder to fool than most. So he was careful only to let me see him in shadow and whenever possible he kept his hand over his mouth and chin. However, I realise that none of this would count as evidence; any more, I suppose, than that much more careless oversight I noticed when you and I were making our tour of inspection this evening, Angie.'

'What was that? I don't recall your mentioning it.'

'There was no point. Not being what you'd call house-proud yourself and not being acquainted with Mrs Cheeseman, who is meticulous to the point of neurosis, you simply did not notice that in grabbing your suitcase off the bed, where she had placed it when your brother brought it round, you had rumpled the counterpane and pulled it sideways.'

'I am rapidly getting out of my depth again,' Toby complained. 'Would it be possible to come to the point?'

'Yes, by all means. We are approaching the climax now. The minute Angie denies something or proves me wrong, I shall stop. Until then I propose to carry on and tell you what really happened this evening. It shouldn't take long, but why don't we move to more comfortable surroundings and have a drink? Or would you prefer more coffee, Angie?'

'Yes, please. I think it behoves me to stick to coffee.'

Judging by his expression, this remark did more than any words of mine to convince Robin that she and I were in deadly earnest and the battle was now joined.

I made enough for six cups, having foreseen that Robin and Toby would already have moved on to the whisky by the time I brought it in and, having placed the first of them

175

on the table beside Angie, I said, 'There is no way of telling how much similarity there was between your encounter with Tom on the doorstep and the way you described it, but I feel sure that what happened afterwards went something like this: you came inside, slammed the door behind you, saw the keys, read the message and got a pretty clear picture of what had been going on. However, there was no time to act on it then or even make a plan because you could hear me bleating from in here. So you came in and got to work on releasing my bonds. I think you may also have saved my life by turning up when you did, incidentally, and I'm sorry I forgot to thank you.'

'There was no need. The cords must have been uncomfortable, but they could hardly have proved fatal.'

'On the other hand, and this may be on the border line between fact and fiction, I did feel something in the nature of a cloth or scarf being rammed up against my face. It could hardly have been intended for a gag, since there was no one else in the house. So it's just possible that what he had in mind was a neat job of strangling or suffocation, disguised as the work of a burglar who had overstepped the mark. In fact, I hardly see what other purpose he could have had in coming here at all.'

'Do hurry up and get to the bit about Mrs Cheeseman and the rumpled bed,' Toby said. 'That's the one I'm curious about.'

'So you should be because it has a connection with your arrival. When I let you in it suddenly came to me that the bed had looked exactly as it does when you have unpacked your suitcase and pulled it on to the floor. So then I realised how Tom had got in and why it had taken Angie so long to get through to you on the telephone, Robin.'

'You keep starting by clearing up mysteries and ending with fresh ones,' he complained. 'What have I got to do with it?'

'Angie was out of the room for nearly ten minutes,

despite the fact that she had your special, secret extension number, which usually works like a charm. So obviously most of that time was being used for something else. Patching up Tom's mistakes, in other words, which is the way she has spent, or some might say wasted, so much of her life.'

'What patching up was needed this time?' Robin asked, adding, 'I apologise for talking about you as though you were not here, Angie, but we seem to have no choice.'

She nodded but did not speak and I took up the tale again: 'We can assume that earlier today she and Tom had met in London. She had her suitcase with her and she told him that she had arranged to bring it here before four o'clock and collect the keys, so that she could, if necessary, let herself in before Robin or I came home. However, she was running late and would not have time for any of this. So then it fell out, either at his suggestion or hers, that Tom would at least relieve her of the case by dropping it off here on his way to Victoria Station to catch his train.'

'It was my suggestion, as it happens,' Angie said, making her first, modest contribution.

'I felt sure it had been,' I told her. 'Making suggestions to Tom has always come naturally to you and he has usually fallen in with them. Unfortunately, not always, though. There have been one or two occasions in his life when he has acted on his own initiative and they have always ended in disaster. This evening's was no exception.'

'To some extent, that is true,' she admitted.

'So you're not denying it?' Robin asked.

'Denying what?'

'Well, if I've got it right, you don't deny that he did deliver the suitcase, explaining to Mrs Cheeseman that he was your brother, and she handed over the keys according to instructions. Whereupon, on impulse, presumably, he

177

put them in his pocket and an hour or so later used them to ransack this room?'

'There would be no point in denying it, since you have only to ask Mrs Cheeseman in the morning.'

'And I am grateful to you for making that unnecessary,' I assured her. 'All the same, you did try to cover up for him, so long as you believed there was a chance of getting away with it. The first thing you did, while ostensibly trying to get through to Robin, was to dispose of the top sheet of the message pad, hoping that, had I read it, the memory would have been wiped out by subsequent events. The second was to streak upstairs to the top floor, drag your suitcase off the bed and place it beside the front door, where, of course, it should have been at that point in our lives.'

'Yes, perfectly true,' she said impatiently, as though growing tired at last of her passive role. 'He behaved very badly and with criminal stupidity, but he's not a thief. Nothing has been stolen.'

'I think perhaps you are being a little stupid now,' Toby remarked, 'in reminding us of that.'

'Do you? Why?'

'What Toby means, I suppose,' Robin explained, 'is that you have brought all three of us to the point of asking exactly what he was doing here, if not to pinch something?'

'Don't include me in that,' I said, 'because I can guess. With the keys in his hand, the temptation to return when there was no one here was too strong to resist.'

'Yes, but what for?'

'To kill me, I expect.'

'Why, though, Tessa? What had you done?'

'Made him feel frightened and insecure. I was finding out too much and somehow or other he had to stop me. Mind you, I doubt if he'd have gone through with it. I don't imagine that murder comes naturally to him any

178

more than theft, but it was certainly in his mind when he came here this evening and that's why this room was ransacked. He was trying to ensure that when the deed was discovered it would look like the work of a common-or-garden burglar and not some fear-crazed religious freak. It's a sad story, whichever way you look at it. A good but weak man whose life has been dominated and ultimately destroyed by three strong-minded women.'

'Three?' Angie enquired. 'You surely don't include Dodie or Baba?'

'No, but I do include his wife. She played a different sort of role from yours and Laura's, but her influence was just as powerful. Perhaps more so, in a sense, because she managed to see you both off and to become for several years the one dominant force in his life. I suppose he was able to keep going tolerably well, so long as one faction or the other was in control. It was only when there was a major conflict of interest between the two that things really began to fall apart and that, of course, is why Beryl was murdered and why her disappearance was not reported. Next of kin had the best of reasons for keeping it dark.'

I paused here, waiting for a reaction to this announcement, which was slow in coming, but made up for it in intensity. Angie was the first to speak:

'But that's ridiculous! I do hope you're not insinuating that it was Beryl who died in the fire?'

'Then I must dash those hopes,' I told her, 'because, sorry as I am in so many ways, that is precisely what I am doing.'

'Then you're out of your mind. She's been dead for nearly two years.'

'So you told me, but I didn't quite believe it then and I don't now. It just didn't ring true because when Derek was telling Robin and me your family history and how Baba was threatening to stir it all up again by publishing her autobiography he never said a word about Beryl having died. Considering how disastrous Tom's marriage had been, from Laura's point of view, having cut her off so completely from her beloved baby brother, surely it's inconceivable that his wife's death would have passed without comment from her and without Pam and Derek hearing about it? Furthermore, Angie, it was the one subject on which you made a couple of slips yourself.'

'Did I indeed? When was that?'

'During our conversation at Beachclyffe that afternoon. Very wisely, you stuck as close to the truth as you could, but at one point you told me that Beryl had become more eager than ever to grab a share of the limelight when your father's plays started to come back into fashion. That struck me as odd because, in fact, it was a comparatively recent development and, if Beryl had really been dead for two years, she wouldn't have been alive to see it. I let it pass, but then, almost immediately afterwards, you said that, so far, Tom seemed not to have suffered any remorse as a result of his wife's death, which was going a bit too far. I was about to point out that, two years on, there couldn't any longer be much to worry about on that score, but you saw it coming just in time and pretended to have been talking about something else.'

'Even so, it does nothing to connect her with the woman who died in the fire and may I remind you that neither you nor anyone else can ever know for certain who she was?'

'I'm not so sure. Admittedly, that was true when there was nothing to work on except charred rags and bones, but I imagine the situation might change if the experts had some lead to her identity. Robin will have to confirm it for us, but I believe that a scrap of clothing or strand of hair would be more than enough to establish whether they had belonged to one particular woman.'

'And if, by some extraordinary chance, it could be proved that Beryl was still alive and had somehow got into the house that night, it still would not alter the fact that Tom was miles away from the place before and during the fire.'

'No, but I'm not talking exclusively about Tom, as it happens.'

'Oh?'

'No, as I said before, I don't see him as the stuff that murderers are made of and I'm certain that neither you nor Laura would have trusted him to carry out such a tricky and dangerous job on his own. He would inevitably have gummed it up.'

'Then what has all this been leading up to? Surely not to the suggestion that Dodie and I were responsible?'

'Well, not Dodie, obviously, since everyone knows she was in Denmark at the time. From what I hear, there are other factors to rule her out so we may as well get that straight while we're about it. Am I right in saying that, despite what you told us, or allowed us to believe, Dodie knew nothing about the forged letters and all that went with them? I imagine you will answer truthfully, seeing that she's no longer here to defend herself?'

She did not answer at all, but Robin had a question:

'What makes you think Dodie had nothing to do with it?'

'Well, we never met, but there was one thing I heard about her several times from several sources. She had a reputation for being vague and vacillating and it was also mentioned that she spent a large part of her life on the telephone, acting as the family go-between and passing on the news about each member to all the others. So it's almost inconceivable that she would have been trusted with a secret of that nature. She'd have given it away in the first ten minutes, out of sheer forgetfulness, if nothing else. In passing, though, I'd say that, since her death

181

resulted from panic, anxiety and distress, she had gradually begun to piece together what had been going on and how she had been used in the deception. However, perhaps it's all irrelevant in the context of Beryl's murder, so let's go back to that.

'I'll start with the assumption that she'd read, or been told about the newspaper story which revealed that Baba had miraculously found herself in possession of a bundle of letters written by her father at the height of his fame to a young woman half his age and containing some startling disclosures about his private life. Neither Mallings nor the girl herself was referred to by name, but Beryl would have known all about Tom's skill in forgery and doubtless cottoned on to the truth pretty quickly. After that it would simply have been a matter of getting someone, maybe a friend at the hospital where they'd both worked, to find out as much as she could about where he went and what he was up to. I expect she learnt enough by that means to confirm her suspicions and so she wrote to Tom, saying that unless he gave in to her demands and accepted her terms she would tell Baba everything. How does that sound to you, so far?'

'Not bad at all,' Angie admitted, her composure now restored. 'It is rather the kind of thing she would have done, so it's plausible enough, so long as you accept the original premise.'

'And would you find it equally plausible to suggest that in her letter to Tom she also offered to meet him somewhere on neutral ground, so that they could discuss it?'

'Why not?'

'And also that, on Laura's advice perhaps, he replied that the meeting could take place at the cottage which his half-sister had rented for the summer and where he was acting as caretaker during her absence abroad?'

'I find it hard to believe that anyone would make an appointment of that kind in the middle of the night, but no

182

matter. It is not the trimmings of your imaginative reconstruction which concern me, but the implication that any of us three could have taken part in it. That, if I may say so, is where it comes unstuck.'

Up to this point it had been a much smoother ride than I had anticipated, since, while not admitting much, she had not, until now, denied anything either. So, with everything to win or lose, I drew a deep breath:

'You may say it as often as you like, Angie, but I shan't agree with you.'

'Really? You expect to prove that all three of us had set ourselves up with false alibis for that night? You won't find it easy.'

'I don't have to prove anything of the kind. All your alibis are unexceptionable, as far as they go, but not one of them goes far enough. In the first place, there was no need whatever to make an appointment in the dead of night. Beryl could just as easily have been murdered between, say, four and five in the afternoon. No one would ever be able to state that she had been dead for more than six hours when the fire started.'

'Maybe not, but quite a strain on the nerves hanging around with a corpse all that time. Risky, too, I'd have thought.'

'There was no need to hang around, Angie, that's what I'm driving at. It would have been idiotic because if by some remote chance anyone had called at the house during the interval he certainly wouldn't have wanted to be found on the premises. Furthermore, it was essential to get home and establish an alibi for the next part of the programme.'

'So you are accusing Tom, after all?'

'When I say he, you must take it to mean he or she because, according to my theory, this was a threefold operation. None of you possesses an alibi to cover the whole of it, but each could have played a separate key role.'

'I think I must interrupt here,' Robin said, 'before you get too carried away. As I recall, the fire started somewhere between midnight and two a.m., but Angie has witnesses to say that she was still in Gloucestershire at ten or thereabouts and it would have taken her at least four hours to drive over to Mallings.'

'Which simply means that she could have passed by the house soon after two o'clock in the morning, to verify that it was burning up nicely and that no fire engines had so far reached the scene.'

'But that is by the way and, as for Laura and Tom, we know they must both have been at Beachclyffe throughout the period because of those two telephone calls from Pam, one at ten thirty and the other just after midnight.'

'Yes, that was a fortunate coincidence and not easy to have planned in advance. Although I daresay Laura would have been capable of putting in a couple of calls to Pam herself, had it been necessary, and the chances that it wouldn't be were very high. I bet Derek would tell you that there are very few bedtimes these days when Pam doesn't call her mother on the telephone. I should guess too that it was particularly likely to happen when Laura was out of London and that she wouldn't hesitate to do so in the middle of the night.'

Robin acknowledged the truth of this with a resigned nod and I said, 'So if you're all set now, I'll give you the run down, as I see it, and you can all decide if I'm right and, if so, what should be done about it.'

'I know what I shall do about it,' Toby said. 'Having come through so far, I shall hear you out to the bitter end and then return to my lodgings. Any other sort of decision would be quite beyond me.'

'To make it as short as I can, then, some time between five and six that evening, having seen Dodie off at Gatwick, which was the signal for the curtain to rise on the last act, Laura arrived at Mallings. She left her car some

184

distance away and walked to Fairview. When Beryl arrived to keep her appointment with Tom she was dealt with in such a way as to put her out of action, at least for six or seven hours. Laura then returned to her car and drove to Beachclyffe, where she remained indoors until the next morning.

'About two hours later Pam rang up. Tom answered and passed it over to Laura. Soon afterwards he went out, borrowing Laura's car and not returning until one or one thirty in the morning.'

Angie opened her mouth to speak, but Robin got in first:

'Now this is where you fall down, Tess. It was around midnight when Pam called for the second time and the same thing happened. Tom answered when it rang. That is too easily checked to be an invention.'

'You only think so because there are two things about Laura that you don't yet know. Or rather, one you don't know and one you've forgotten.'

'What have I forgotten?'

'That, ostensibly, the only reason for Laura being at Beachclyffe at all and not holding Pam's hand was that Tom was recovering from a bad cold. What you didn't know was that she'd done a year's training at RADA, where she gained a reputation as a mimic. Put those two facts together and you'll soon see how it was worked.'

'And you seriously believe that Laura was a party to all this?'

'I'm afraid so, Robin. All three of them had so much to lose, you see, if Beryl carried out her threat, but Laura would have been worst hit of all because she'd built up a solid reputation for herself and Baba hated that. She'd have done anything to see it collapse and she'd have been merciless in getting her revenge. It wouldn't have done Derek much good either.'

'I daresay it won't do him an awful lot of good to find

185

himself married to the daughter of a murderess, come to that.'

'I don't think it will come to that. Perhaps I'm an optimist, but I'm banking on—'

I broke off here because, with masterly stage management, the telephone had started to ring.

'Might be for you,' I told Angie, but she was already out of her seat and halfway to the door.

EIGHTEEN

'How good it is,' I remarked a few days later, at the conclusion of a brutally competitive and acrimonious game of croquet, 'to be back in the peace and solitude of the country, where everything is in its right place and the old values still count.'

It was the sight of Robin packing the balls and mallets back in their boxes, as Toby subsided exhausted into a garden chair and Mrs Parkes came tripping over the grass towards us, which had inspired this reflection, but he was not in a mood to agree.

'Your trouble, Tessa, is that you're immature. You're as bad as Tom.'

'What a dreadful thing to say! And, anyway, I thought marriage to you had changed all that?'

'Not at all. You still love to dip your baby fingers in some murky pool, stir up a few lives and then go merrily on your way when you've had enough.'

I was speechless with rage and astonishment, but, for once, Toby roused himself and rallied to my support.

'I think you need a drink, Robin. It must be early symptoms of dehydration which make you round on her like this. Oh, thank you so much, Mrs Parkes.'

'I am not rounding on her. It is the way I usually face and I was thinking particularly of her behaviour the other night. Imagine stringing us along like that and spinning it out long enough for matters to take the course which Angie was hoping for! No wonder she never argued or complained while Tessa was hurling accusations about. She was quite content to sit there and let you and me suffer while she watched the hours go by. It was as though they were both playing some childish, secret game.'

'Oh, yes, indeed, very foolish and irresponsible, my dear, but at least they both knew what they were up to and how to get their own way. It probably just goes to show that most women are congenitally immature, but I still consider it rather unfair to compare them to Tom.'

'Oh, he's another case! All that sitting around cross-legged and chanting meaningless invocations. Nothing to do with religion, just a way of shutting out reality. It's all so—'

'Immature?'

'Precisely! And then, when some real crisis is staring him in the face and won't leave him alone, however much he hides, what does he do? Lashes out like some tormented bull and murders whoever it is who's causing all the trouble.'

'I blame Sheridan Seymour for most of it,' I said. 'Every one of his descendants seems to have been either mentally or emotionally stunted, so the bad streak must have come from him. All the same, you will admit that they inherited some of their respective mothers' good qualities as well and Tom acquitted himself rather splendidly in the last act. Taking the whole blame for everything, including his wife's death, and then putting a nice, tidy end to himself was quite a grown-up way to do it.'

'Was it a nice, tidy end?' Toby asked. 'I didn't hear how he did it.'

'Slashed his wrists,' I replied. 'He telephoned Angie after dinner that evening, as you remember, she having already warned him that the game was up, and read out the confession he'd been writing to the coroner while we were sitting round the dining room table. After that he retired to the bathroom and went to work with the carving knife. He knew just what to do and how to do it. His hospital work had brought him into contact with too

188

many failed suicides to make any of the usual mistakes.'

'Efficient, I grant you,' Robin said, 'but I don't subscribe to the view that there was anything noble about it. He was due for a long spell of imprisonment, in any case, and dragging his sisters down with him wouldn't have done anything to alleviate that situation, even if they were morally responsible.'

'That's just what I meant. Some men, specially the immature type like Tom, might have tried to shove some of the blame on them, if not all of it, but in fact the last act of his life was designed to protect them. And we should be grateful to him, you know. The full story of those bogus letters will never be made public now and nor will the Seymour/Lampeter history be dragged out again. So Derek and Pam will be able to live happy ever after, with only the occasional miscarriage to relieve the tedium. How are they getting on, by the way?'

'Not bad, all things considered. Laura's gone abroad, as I probably told you. She's starting work on a new book about one of those Hanoverian princesses and she needs to spend several months in Germany doing her research. That's the story, anyway.'

'And a neat one, in my opinion. What do you say, Toby?'

'Although perhaps not very popular with Pam. Or Derek either, I daresay, since he'll presumably be faced with some pretty hefty telephone bills.'

'Apparently not,' Robin admitted with a hint of reluctance. 'It seems that Laura gave Pam a bit of a straight talk before she left. Told her it was about time she grew up and worried less about herself and more about Derek's well-being, peace of mind and so forth. Early days, of course, but so far it's having some effect. At any rate, there hasn't been any talk of a miscarriage for the past forty-eight hours, which he's inclined to see as the breakthrough.'

'He expects it to last?'

'I think he does. He's never been able to see any fault in that silly girl and he now takes the attitude that her mother was to blame for those unfortunate little bouts of nerves and hysteria. It was Laura's cosseting and over-protectiveness which did all the damage and, now that she's cut the umbilical cord at last and removed herself from the centre of their lives, everything's going to be all right.'

'There could be a grain of truth lurking there,' I said, 'and, if this child ever does manage to get born the right side up, with everything in place, it might mark the beginning of a new era for that family. With a bit of luck, plus a nice, sensible, unimaginative father like Derek in the background, it could turn out to be quite normal. It might even grow up without dreams of becoming a star of stage and screen.'

'Oh, I don't know, I think you're being rather hard on your profession there. There could be worse dreams to grow up with. Don't you agree, Toby?'

'No.'

'Well, I do,' I said, 'and I'm grateful to you, Robin. It's the first civil thing you've said to me for three days.'

'I was only thinking that, with any luck, this one won't grow up with dreams of becoming a star of stage and screen and an amateur detective on the side. That's when the real trouble begins.'

AAO-1963